# Susannah stepped inside the house.

It enveloped her in its watchful hush. She had grown accustomed to the wind outside—its absence intensified the waiting quiet. Susannah felt more like a curious and slightly frightened daughter than a professional architect. Here, in this house all alone, her mother had died—little more than a week ago.

Susannah began to move as if in a dream. She attended only to the feeling that drew her from room to room and, finally, to a broad staircase shrouded in darkness.

She climbed the staircase as if in a trance. At the second floor, Susannah stopped. Her heart beat like thunder. A s̲ ̲ ̲ ̲ of light pierced through the storm clouds an̲ ̲ ̲ ̲ ̲ ̲ ̲ ̲ ̲ ̲ ̲ ̲ ̲ windows, falling in a pale ̲ ̲ ̲

"Mother?"

A sharp noise ̲ ̲ ̲ ̲ ̲ ̲ ̲ ̲ ̲ ̲ ̲ ̲ ̲ ̲ ̲ ̲ ̲ ̲ ̲ ̲ ight disappeared and Susannan ̲ ̲ ̲ ̲ ̲ ̲ ̲ ̲ ̲ ̲ ̲ oot-steps, loud and heavy, sounded below.

She backed herself into the farthest corner of the hall as the footsteps came up the stairs.

## ABOUT THE AUTHOR

Madelyn Sanders lives in North Carolina. The things she finds most fascinating in life are her writing, large bodies of water and old houses. In *Laird's Mount*, her third novel for Harlequin Intrigue, she left out the water and concentrated on the old house.

## Books by Madelyn Sanders

# Laird's Mount

## Madelyn Sanders

## *Harlequin Books*

TORONTO • NEW YORK • LONDON
AMSTERDAM • PARIS • SYDNEY • HAMBURG
STOCKHOLM • ATHENS • TOKYO • MILAN
MADRID • WARSAW • BUDAPEST • AUCKLAND

I want to thank Todd Dickinson and Tahti Carter, both of whom were essential in making this book a reality. Todd, of Dickinson Restorations, is a restoration contractor par excellence. Tahti was my editor. I also thank Bill Crowther for his help on my visits to the property that inspired this book.

Harlequin Intrigue edition published July 1993

ISBN 0-373-22234-3

LAIRD'S MOUNT

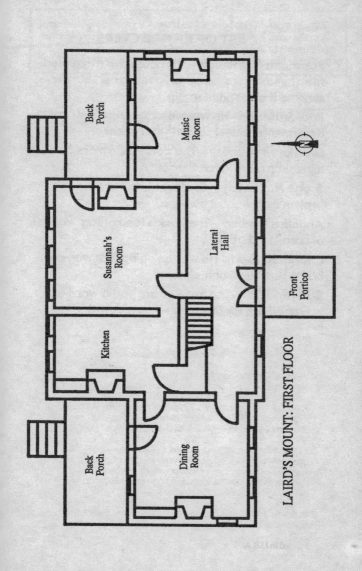

LAIRD'S MOUNT: FIRST FLOOR

# CAST OF CHARACTERS

**Susannah Hathaway**—The house she'd inherited from her mother seemed to speak to her, but the sentiment wasn't maternal.

**Paul Starbuck**—He was restoring Laird's Mount to its former grandeur, but at what price?

**Dr. Marvin Bradley**—This doctor had more on his mind than his next tonsillectomy.

**Judge Hathaway**—Susannah's father was a broken man without his wife.

**Angelica Herbert**—The bank's loan officer was full of unsolicited advice.

**Charlie Herbert**—He was an aging jock with an itch to buy Susannah's house.

**Barbara Blair**—The town gossip had a word or two of advice for Susannah—leave town!

# Chapter One

Susannah Hathaway sat curled on her couch, long arms clasped around long legs, her chin resting on her upthrust knees. She was brooding—a most unusual occupation for Susannah.

Suddenly her head snapped up, she let go of her legs, and her right hand flew to a spot behind her right ear. "Damn!" she swore aloud, rubbing hard. A pain, hot and piercing, bit into her. Just as quickly as it came, it was gone.

"What in the world..." she muttered. An insect bite? But there were no insects in Cambridge, Massachusetts, in the middle of winter, the cold killed them all. A spider, then? "Yech!" she said, swatting at her hair, brushing at the shoulders of the gray sweat suit she wore. Intellectually, Susannah could appreciate spiders; but when it came to the possibility of having one crawl around on her—well, that was a different story.

She jumped up off the couch and shook her head hard enough to mess up her hair, but still no spider tumbled out. She unzipped her top, took it off and shook it. No spider. But she was convinced she'd been bitten and felt weak in the knees.

*It is probably poisonous,* she thought with a gloominess that matched her mood. Susannah trooped off to the bathroom, wearing only her bra, with her top trailing from one hand. Leaning toward the mirror over the sink, she held her hair back and looked at the place from which the pain had seemed to come. No red spot, nothing. But just to be sure, she hung her head and brushed her hair hard over the sink, wincing as the brush took a tangle too vigorously. She brushed until her scalp tingled. Gradually, the rhythmic brushing calmed her.

Finally Susannah straightened up and flipped her hair back into place. She felt its soft, curved-under ends touch her shoulders as she looked into the sink: a few honey gold strands lay on the white porcelain, that was all. No spider.

"Know what your problem is?" she asked her image in the mirror. "You're getting morbid, that's what. Developing psychosomatic spider bites, for God's sake! That's what comes of sitting around moping on a perfectly good Saturday afternoon. You should get on with your life. Do something. Go for a run!"

It seemed like good advice, even considering the source. Susannah shrugged back into her top and zipped it. The wide-apart eyes that looked back at her from the mirror were gray. The December sky outside was gray. Her whole life felt gray, in spite of the pep talk. She was dissatisfied with her work, and she had just ended a relationship with a man she'd thought she loved.

Nevertheless, she was going to run. Before leaving the bathroom she leaned toward the mirror, lifted her hair and looked behind her right ear one last time. Still nothing, no red spot. The weakness in her legs was gone.

"A good run will cure anything," she pronounced, and went to look for her running shoes.

An hour and a half later, Susannah returned to her apartment. She had run along the banks of the Charles River until the day ran out of light, and was feeling marginally better even though she hadn't achieved the runner's high she craved—the reason she was addicted to running. She turned on lights and shed layers of clothing as she made her way to the bedroom. In the blackness of the unlit room the red message light on the answering machine was blinking.

*It will be bad news, I know it will be bad news,* Susannah thought, *I've felt it coming all day.* Her heart went up into her throat and left a hollow space in her chest. She didn't turn on the light. Slowly she walked over to the answering machine and touched the button. The message was a command from her father: "Susannah, call as soon as you get in. It's important."

She flipped on the light on the bedside table that held the telephone and answering machine, sat on the edge of the bed, opened the drawer in the table and took out her address book. She had to look up her parents' number. They were retired now—or rather

Judge Harold Hathaway was; his wife, Jane, Susannah's mother, had never worked—and they had moved South, to a small town in Virginia, near the North Carolina border. Susannah had not yet been there and had not called often enough in the two years since their move to know the number by heart. The simple truth was that the Judge and Jane loved each other so exclusively that there was no love left to give their only child, which was not Susannah's fault. But it had taken adulthood and three years of therapy for her to figure that out.

Her hand trembled as she reached for the receiver, and she stopped in midmotion. She took several deep breaths to calm herself. *The Judge never calls, Mother does,* she thought. Her hair, disarrayed by the long run, hung in her eyes, and she tossed her head to fling it back. Her mind was crowded with images: her father's face, handsome in an austere way, with his tall, long-boned body. Her mother's heart-shaped face, almost too pretty, and her tiny, fragile form. Throughout her lonely childhood Susannah had watched herself grow taller and taller, every year looking more and more like her father, right down to the color of her hair and the very shape and shade of her gray eyes...yet she'd longed to be small and pretty like her mother. That she had also inherited her father's intellect and strong will had never been much consolation.

That strength of will made Susannah take the phone in hand and dial. She heard her father say, "Susannah, you'll have to come. Your mother died this afternoon. My Jane is gone."

IN ONLY A FEW SHORT DAYS, Susannah's life became a baffling maze of grief. She knew of no way to comfort her father, who was even more baffled and grief stricken than she. The Judge had worn his courtroom persona throughout the funeral, but afterward he collapsed inward, into himself, like the implosion of a stately old building. At age seventy-eight he became like a child, wandering the rooms of his new house as if he did not know where he was, forgetting to sleep, forgetting to eat, forgetting to change his clothes. The only thing Susannah knew clearly was that she could not leave the Judge alone, not until he was better.

Meanwhile Susannah had her own problems to solve, her own peace to make. What tortured her most was the unfinished family business. Jane Hathaway had died on the tenth of December, two weeks short of a Christmas visit that Susannah had been planning for months. In Susannah's mind that visit would have been a reconciliation and a new beginning. She had intended to tell her mother many things—the most important was, *I love you, Mother.*

Perhaps Jane Hathaway, too, felt that things were unfinished between her and her daughter...because she seemed to be trying to come back from beyond the grave. Night after night Susannah's mother invaded her sleep. She came in a strange dream that was more like a vision: Jane's heart-shaped face, surrounded by a halo of silvery hair, floated bodiless in black space, mouth open and shaped for speech, eyes wide as if in surprise. Or fear. Closer and closer the face would come, zooming larger and larger until it filled the screen of Susannah's dream. With the vision came a sense of unbearable urgency. Jane wanted to speak, to tell her daughter something, something terribly important. But she did not.

What was her mother trying to tell her?

Five days after the funeral, a lawyer came from Boston to read Jane Hathaway's will. The Judge once more put on his courtroom persona. Susannah, who had not thought about her mother even having a will, received a jolt. Jane had been a wealthy woman in her own right, a fact she had never told her daughter. She had left everything to Susannah, including the old house she'd bought and was in the process of restoring at the time of her death. The old house in which she'd died: Laird's Mount.

After the reading of the will the Judge receded again into his grief. Susannah felt more baffled and lost than ever, but that night, when she awoke from the dream in the usual cold sweat and tangled bedclothes, four words lingered in Susannah's mind: *Go to Laird's Mount!*

The next day, she went.

Laird's Mount proved to be hard to find. It certainly wasn't on the beaten path—though the only path Susannah had beat since coming to Kinloch was from her father's house to the grocery store and back. The town of Kinloch, Virginia, was so small that she'd figured she didn't need directions, and anyway, there was no one to ask except the Judge and she hadn't wanted to do that. The street address should have been enough. But she drove her mother's car up St. Andrews Road and back down without seeing a single house that looked old and in need of restoration. On her third pass, Susannah began to read the numbers on the mailboxes that lined the side of the road.

There! A mailbox with the right number—but no house! Beside the mailbox was a gravel driveway that looked like more of a track. The two houses on either side of it had their own mailboxes and driveways, and she couldn't sit with the car idling forever, so she turned into the gravel track and followed it. Beyond the backyards of the two houses the track curved sharply to the left, then to the right, and Susannah braked to a stop.

The atmosphere felt suddenly quite different. A pair of tall, crumbling brick pillars held a still-sturdy but rusting iron gate, which stood open. To either side stretched a barrier wall of ancient cedars, drooping dark, shaggy evergreen foliage as far to the right and left as her eyes could see. The effect, no doubt calculated by the one who had planted the trees and erected the gates long ago, was forbidding. Susannah gripped the steering wheel with white knuckles and drove on.

Gradually a vista opened up, a scene of astonishing beauty. Broad, sweeping lawns, now ill kept and winter brown, rose gently to where the house crowned the highest point. The house itself was some distance away so its features were not immediately apparent, but

Susannah could see that it was very tall, its lines were classically simple, and it was built of brick.

As she gazed at Laird's Mount, set like a jewel in its landscape, Susannah's days of confusion and loss faded into the background. She stopped being a guilty, overgrown child and became once more the competent professional woman that she really was: Susannah Hathaway, architect, MIT graduate, at age thirty, the only female member of a Cambridge, Massachusetts, architectural firm. She beheld the house with the eyes of a master designer and she drove on eagerly, ready to see more.

The gravel drive approached to within about a hundred yards of the house and then curved to the right. At the curve point was an old mounting block and a lamppost that marked the end of a long brick walk to the front door. Susannah continued up the drive until it stopped near a ramshackle wooden shed whose function must once have been to house carriages, then cars, but now was within a hairbreadth of falling down. She parked and got out, walked a few steps and stopped to admire the view, which was even more impressive from this perspective.

Acres and acres of lawn rolled away downhill. The man who'd built this house, a Scotsman to judge by the "Laird," had placed his dwelling in the highest seat. The sky seemed close here. Clouds massed overhead, their shapes quickly changing, moving, driven by a rising wind that scoured her cheeks and tossed her hair. Susannah turned, scanning the sky. She was not sure of her direction but thought the house had a north-south orientation, and if so, then the ever-growing bank of dark purple clouds was moving in from the west. A storm was coming, not snow—the temperature, while brisk, was not cold enough—but certainly rain.

Just beyond the ramshackle wooden structure where she'd parked was a little building made of the same brick as the main house. Remembering her history of American architecture, Susannah labeled the small building a dependency—probably a kitchen. Because of the hot, humid climate, wealthy Southerners in past centuries had kept their kitchens separate from their main houses. She would have liked to look into the small building to determine its function for certain, but the day was darkening by the second; that could wait until later. The big old house was her first priority.

First she circled the building from the outside in a critical appraisal. The bricks were deep red, darkened with age, and most were in good condition. The proportions of the house were impressive; its height made it seem larger than it actually was. The style was Federal, massive and severe in its lack of ornamentation. The main block rose forty to fifty feet, although judging by the windows it was only two-and-a-half stories—the rooms inside would have very high ceilings. The two side blocks, identical to each other, were one-and-a-half stories. The windows had the many small panes typical of the period, and most of them were intact, though their outside shutters were not. All the exterior woodwork needed both paint and repair.

The dark gray roof appeared to be slate, and in good condition.

Finally coming to the front door, Susannah fished her mother's keys from her purse. There was a new lock, its brass incongruously bright in the door's old, deeply carved wood paneling. The key worked smoothly. Susannah stepped inside.

The old house enveloped Susannah in its watchful hush. She had grown accustomed to the wind outside—its absence intensified the waiting quiet. Now the professional architect who had critically appraised the outside of Laird's Mount disappeared. In her place stood a curious and slightly frightened daughter. Susannah remembered the real reason she had come to Laird's Mount. Here, in this house, all alone, Jane Hathaway had died . . . only a little more than a week ago.

Susannah began to move as if she herself were in a dream. She walked through high-ceilinged empty spaces peopled by moving shadows, shadows that shifted and changed with the changing light of the brewing storm. She noted none of the architectural details that would usually fascinate her, she attended only to a feeling that drew her from doorway to doorway until she was back where she had started . . . and then, the feeling drew her to a broad staircase.

Up and up she went, and with every step the hushed house closed around her, drawing her on. When she reached the second floor, Susannah stopped. She stood in a large, lofty hall. Her heart beat like thunder. For a single moment a shaft of light pierced through the storm clouds and shone through the tall windows, illuminating dust motes in the air, falling in a pale rectangle upon the floor.

Susannah whispered, "Mother?"

*Wham!* A sharp noise split the silence, reverberated through the walls. The shaft of light disappeared. Susannah froze in fright. Footsteps—loud, heavy— sounded below. *Tramp, tramp, tramp, tramp!*

Susannah backed into the middle of the large, square hall, fighting down panic. Suddenly she, normally the most logical and unsuperstitious person, was thinking of ghosts that slammed doors and tramped with heavy invisible feet through the rooms of old houses. She continued to back up, eyes wide with fright and fastened upon the staircase she'd just ascended. The footsteps were down there. And now they were on the stairs, treading heavily.

She backed herself into the farthest corner of the hall as the footsteps came closer. The storm began in earnest, flinging rain sharp as pebbles at the windowpanes. A dark shape gathered on the edge of Susannah's peripheral vision, and along with it, a sense that she was not alone in the hall. Yet the footsteps were on the stairs, dead ahead. She was torn, but she turned her head and looked. The dark shape loomed on another, smaller, ascending stairway—and as Susannah spied it, the shape dissolved right before her eyes.

There was no time to ponder this strangeness. The footsteps were louder, heavier, closer on the main stairway. A head emerged, neck, shoulders, arms— Susannah held her breath. This was no ghost, this was a real man. A real man who immediately saw her and exclaimed, "What the hell..."

She immediately changed her stance from victim to owner as she stepped out of the shadows. She knew she could deal with what she could see and feel.

"My God, woman," he said irreverently, "how the hell did you get in here? You scared the fire out of me!"

"I got in with my key," she replied calmly, walking slowly toward him. The closer she got, the more he seemed familiar, one of the many people she'd met in the blur of her mother's funeral. "I'm Susannah Hathaway, and I own this house. So," she intentionally imitated, "who the *hell* are you?"

"Oh, jeez," he said, half turning away and running a big hand through black, curly hair that was a little too long. He turned back and faced her. "I'm Paul Starbuck. I should have recognized you. I'm sorry, but you were way over there in the corner, and it's so dark in here with the storm and all— Anyway, I have a key, too. I got to worrying that all the windows might not be closed when I saw how dark the sky was getting. I was sure we were in for some rain, and it looks like I was right, doesn't it?"

A great swath of rain slammed against the windows, emphasizing his point. "Yes," Susannah agreed. "I guess we'd better check up here. I gather from hearing you walk around that you've already checked the downstairs?"

"Yep." He started off to his left, and Susannah turned to check the rooms on the right, but he reached out and grabbed her arm. "Better stick with me. The electricity isn't on yet, so it's pretty dark in here and there's junk everywhere. Don't want you to trip over something. Come on." He yanked her arm—a little too hard, but this was no time to argue. She followed, and he let go.

Paul Starbuck was a very big man, not to mention strong. He made Susannah feel small, which was not easy to do since she was five feet eleven. He was five or six inches taller, and had very muscular shoulders and arms and—she couldn't help but notice due to his tight jeans—thighs. He moved swiftly and easily, with the grace of a big man who has command over his body. She didn't get a good look at his face, because she had to keep watching her footing as she walked through the rooms, which were as cluttered as he'd said.

"Well," he said when they returned again to the hall, "I guess that was a waste of time. But like they say, better safe than sorry."

Susannah looked at the little stairway and felt a tingle travel down her spine as she remembered the dark shape she'd seen there. "What's up there? Should we check?"

"Nope. That part of the house hasn't been used for years, and it's just full of old junk."

"An attic?"

"Kind of. But it's more than an attic. There are rooms, probably where servants lived or poor relations or whatever. Anyway, when I first went over the house for Jane I found a couple of panes missing from the windows up there, and I covered them. Nobody's been on the third floor since, so— Hey, listen, I'm sorry about your mother."

"I remember who you are now," said Susannah. She was able now to see his face. It was strong, broad-planed, with a high forehead and eyes large and so dark she could not tell their true color. His hair was black as night, and it curled, probably more than he wanted it to, over his forehead and around his ears. His square jaw was shadowed by a dark beard just beneath the surface of the skin. His mouth was wide and mobile, at the moment curving at the corners in the hint of a smile.

She continued, "You're the contractor who was working with my mother. My father told me that you were the person who found her body here the day she died."

His face grew solemn. "That's right. Jane and I had an appointment for three o'clock that afternoon, but she must have gotten here early because... Well, yeah. I found her. I called the rescue squad but she was already gone. I'm sorry."

Susannah looked at the floor while she got control of her feelings. This man could help her, could answer questions her father either hadn't wanted to or was unable to answer. "Thank you. No one has been able to tell me much of anything. Maybe you could tell me where in the house she was when you found her."

Paul turned around and gestured at the floor in front of the tall windows where rain ran down like tears. "There."

Susannah looked and felt again a tingle down her spine—a sudden shaft of light had pointed out that very place earlier. A coincidence, but eerie. Her mother's face from her dreams loomed at the edge of her mind, and she spoke to push it away. "There wasn't anybody else in the house, was there? Could she have met someone before you came? I mean—" She stopped short, not quite able to say what she meant.

He was looking at her curiously, perhaps a shade defensively. "No one else was here. If she had planned to meet anyone else, she never told me."

"No, I—" Susannah shook her head, making her hair swing.

He wouldn't let her continue, interrupting. "If somebody's dead, the police come along with the rescue squad. Maybe you didn't know that—I didn't. Anyway, they came and they asked me a lot of questions. Ms. Hathaway, I liked your mother a lot. Jane was a great person, and she was doing the whole town of Kinloch a favor when she took on the restoration of this house. I specialize in restoration and I know what I'm talking about. I would have done just about anything for Jane. You're thinking there was something, well, peculiar about the way she died, aren't you?"

Susannah lifted her chin so that she could look into Paul's eyes. "I know there was an autopsy. My father was a judge before he retired, he knows about things like that, and he said that when a death is unanticipated, even if there's no suggestion of foul play, there must be an autopsy. The cause of death was cardiac arrest. Her heart just stopped. For no apparent reason."

"And you're not satisfied with that?"

"No, I guess I'm not. I keep thinking that there must have been a reason."

"Yeah, I can understand how you would. Your mother was a lot younger than your father, wasn't she?"

"Yes," Susannah nodded, "twenty years younger. She was only fifty-eight. I asked my father about her general health lately but he—" She stopped unhappily and just shrugged.

Paul scratched his head thoughtfully. Finally he said, "Ms. Hathaway—"

She looked up. "I wish you'd call me Susannah."

"Okay, Susannah, I want you to know right up front that I was with another client until the ten minutes it took me to drive over here, and on the way I made a call from the phone in my truck. That's what I told the police, and I know they checked it out. Also, there's the fact that there wasn't a single mark on your mother's body. I know because I, uh—looked. I didn't touch her or disturb her or anything, but it was just so damn strange, so awful to find her lying there like that."

"She keeps coming back to me. I have these dreams!" The urgency Susannah felt was in her voice and on her face.

Paul stepped closer. "You could talk to her doctor. Make sure she didn't have something wrong that you don't know about. I mean, if your father doesn't want to talk about it."

"I will. Probably there's nothing, but it's so strange."

"Yes," Paul agreed solemnly. "It is strange."

## Chapter Two

Susannah felt like a thief. Her hands moved quickly, quietly, while she kept one ear cocked for sounds beyond the open door. Not that she would be able to hear anything—her parents' entire new house had wall-to-wall carpeting. She was going through her mother's desk, which was in a corner of the master bedroom, and she didn't want her father to catch her.

One side of her mouth quirked up as she realized the irony. Judge Harold Hathaway had been a criminal court judge, considered one of the best in New England up until his retirement. And here was his own daughter, sneaking around his house and harboring suspicions she didn't dare speak to him about. The Judge of all people should have been the first to suspect a crime, and under normal circumstances would have been an excellent source of help. But these were not normal circumstances.

She found what she was looking for—a doctor's bill among the paid receipts. The procedures were coded, and there was no way she could tell what the codes meant or even who had been seen, since the bill was addressed to Mr. and Mrs. Harold Hathaway. But the doctor's name and address were at the top, and that was enough for Susannah. She shoved it into the pocket of her denim skirt and decided on impulse that she wouldn't call, she'd just go to the doctor's office. It was only two days before Christmas, surely not the busiest time of the year, and she didn't feel like going through the whole waiting game of calling for an appointment.

But she was tugged by a new kind of guilt as she reached into the hall closet for her coat. She squared her shoulders and went to her father's study. The room was a replica of his study in their old home, a place she had never been allowed to enter without invitation. Out of old habit she knocked on the open door and called out, "Judge? May I come in?"

He didn't answer. Susannah wondered, not for the first time, if he really hadn't heard her or if he was just acting as if he hadn't. She felt about ten years old as she approached him where he sat, in his leather wing chair in front of the fireplace. A book lay open on his lap, but he wasn't reading, he was staring into the fire. Lost in memories, no doubt. Susannah's heart ached for him. She had difficulty believing that this white-haired old man with the bent shoulders was the same man she had always called Judge rather than Father. Sorrow and age made him less formidable, and she—who had never, ever, thought to call him Daddy—wanted to touch his shoulder and say, "Dad."

She didn't touch him. She sat on the seat edge of the companion chair and said softly, "Judge, may I speak to you for a minute?"

He turned his head slowly and regarded her with bleary eyes. "What do you want, Susannah?"

What did she want? Many things, but she said only, "I'm going downtown for a little while. May I bring you anything? Are there errands I can do?"

"No, thank you. Nothing." The Judge turned back to his contemplation of the fire.

Susannah pushed her hair back nervously. The rejection made her feel like a child again. "I was thinking about, about Christmas. Tomorrow will be Christmas Eve, and I suppose we should . . . I could . . . get a tree, or something. I mean, Mother wouldn't have wanted us to just, just—"

The Judge closed his book with an audible snap. It was the most decisive thing he'd done in a week. "If you want to celebrate Christmas, then I suggest you return to your friends in Cambridge. There will be no festivities in this house. What your mother might or might not have wanted is irrelevant now. She's dead."

"You don't have to keep saying that, I know as well as you do that she's dead!" Susannah was shocked that she could speak to her father that way, but she was also worn out with tiptoeing around as if she had no will of her own. "I'm here because I want to be here, *with you,* and I don't feel like celebrating anything, either. But I'm not sure the way we've both been behaving is good for us."

"Humph!" The Judge glared at her and for a moment looked more like his former self.

Susannah stood up. "I have a lot to do. I'm not sure how long I'll be gone."

"I'm not your keeper, Susannah. Nor are you mine."

*Maybe not,* she thought as she exited with a dignity reminiscent of the Judge himself leaving a courtroom, *but somebody has to find out the truth.*

MARVIN BRADLEY, M.D.—the sign was posted discreetly on the porch of a Victorian house. Not the usual setup for a doctor's office, but Susannah was beginning to realize that Kinloch was a small town full of small surprises. The front door was unlocked, so she entered.

"Hello?" Susannah called out. She stood uncertainly in a narrow center hallway lined with polished dark wood. There was a graceful little desk near the bottom of a long staircase, but no receptionist. The place seemed deserted. A room that looked like a waiting area was to the left, through a wide arch. She went in and sat down to wait, shrugging out of her coat. Ignoring the magazines scattered on a side table, she occupied herself with guessing the layout of the house and how it had been adapted to medical purposes.

She'd concluded that this was actually a pretty interesting use of space, when a door opened and shut somewhere, followed by the sound of footsteps. Susannah called out, "Dr. Bradley?" She got up and went quickly to the archway.

"Oh, hello there. I didn't realize there was anyone here. Do we have an appointment? I'm sorry, I've given my nurse an extra day off to get ready for Christmas." Marvin Bradley wore a doctor's white coat over his white shirt, a maroon tie with a narrow dark stripe and gray trousers. His hair, cut militarily short, was blond going gray. He had rather protuberant pale blue eyes and a long, thin nose in a face that was also long and thin. His mouth, in startling contrast, was as full-lipped and well shaped as any woman's.

"I don't have an appointment," said Susannah. "I was hoping I might talk to you for a few minutes about my mother. She was a former patient of yours."

"And you are?"

"Oh, sorry. I'm Susannah Hathaway." Automatically she held out her hand for a handshake. He took it between both his own. His hands were very soft.

"Ah! Of course—the height, the remarkable resemblance to your father—I should have remembered. I was at dear Jane's funeral. Of course I can take the time to talk with you. Come, my office is directly opposite."

"Thank you," Susannah murmured, extracting her hand.

"It's fortunate that you came today," said the doctor as he slid back a gleaming sliding door, "because I don't have anyone scheduled. So unless there's an emergency—and I don't expect there will be since I just finished with one—we can talk uninterrupted."

The room they entered was circular and occupied the base of a turret. "This is a handsome house," said Susannah appreciatively. "I'm interested in the way you've adapted it. I was guessing that the smaller rooms on this floor have been converted to examining rooms and maybe the kitchen would be the lab space, while you and your family live upstairs? I don't mean to be intrusive—I have a professional interest. I'm an architect."

"Are you really?" Dr. Bradley went behind his desk and indicated that she should take the facing chair. "How splendid! Yes, I confess I have a great fondness for old houses. It was one of my reasons for settling in Kinloch. There are so many fine examples here, all the way back to the Colonial period. This Victorian, with its many small rooms, was ideal for my purposes. You guessed correctly, except for one thing—I live alone upstairs. I'm a bachelor."

Dr. Bradley's full lips pouted prettily giving Susannah the feeling that she was supposed to offer sympathy for his bachelorhood. Before she'd thought of anything to say, he continued.

"Your mother, of course, got the gem of the lot. I quite envied her. I'd tried to purchase Laird's Mount for years and failed. How Jane managed it, I still don't know." For a moment he seemed to forget Susannah's presence. He frowned, picked up a letter opener from the surface of his desk and began to stroke it idly.

Susannah reminded Dr. Bradley, "I wanted to ask you a few questions about her."

"Oh, yes, so you said." He dropped the letter opener, smoothed out his frown and folded his hands together. "Bearing in mind patient confidentiality, of course, I'll give you whatever answers I can."

Susannah felt her heart rate increase and her mouth go dry. She moistened her lips and plunged in. "I've wondered about the autopsy results. You're familiar with them, I'm sure."

Dr. Bradley nodded, raising his light eyebrows.

"Cardiac arrest," said Susannah. "It was so unexpected."

"Death in a woman her age is usually unexpected."

"I wondered if she'd had any health problems I might not have known about. High blood pressure, anything like that?"

The doctor leaned back in his chair and swiveled it away a half turn. Refusing to answer, or just contemplating?

Susannah pushed on. "I found a bill from you, but from that alone I couldn't tell what you saw mother for. Or even if it was her—I suppose you could have seen my father."

"I've seen them both. I'm a family practitioner. But I referred your father to someone else." He didn't turn back to look at her as he said this.

"Was my mother ill, Dr. Bradley?"

"Not really," he replied with unclinical vagueness. He brought the tips of his fingers together, apart, together, apart. Finally he seemed to reach a decision and swiveled back. "You put me in a difficult position, Ms. Hathaway. Let's just say that what I was treating her for had no bearing on the way she died, and leave it at that."

Susannah's heart thumped once, and skipped a beat. "You mean because of confidentiality?"

He nodded.

"But she's dead! Doesn't that put an end to your obligation? She was my mother, surely I have a right to know...!"

"*This* is what you need to know. Jane had no history of heart problems. No hypertension. On her physical examination when she first became my patient, she was given a routine ECG and it was normal. You may be unaware of this, Ms. Hathaway, but there are such things as congenital heart defects that can remain silent all one's life, and then suddenly, poof!" In illustration, he snapped his fingers.

Susannah blinked, startled.

The doctor concluded, "I believe that is what happened to your mother. However, I did not see her body myself, I was never called. An unfortunate oversight in my opinion, as I was her physician. The county coroner was called, instead. If you have any further questions you should talk to him, though I seriously doubt he will tell you as much as I have."

"I'm sure you're right," Susannah mumbled, intensely aware that the man still had not told her what he was treating her mother for. Nor had she missed the fact that he called her mother "Jane" yet referred to her as "Ms. Hathaway." Did that mean anything? Perhaps he called all his patients by their first names.

"How is your father's eyesight?"

The question came at her out of left field. Susannah stammered, "I—I beg your pardon?"

"His cataracts. I see by your expression that he didn't tell you."

Susannah shook her head.

Dr. Bradley sighed. "Just what one might expect of a man like the Judge. Too proud and stubborn to admit he has a problem, medical or otherwise."

That was Susannah's own opinion of her father, but she didn't like to hear it from someone else. She sat up straighter. "I notice you feel no need to protect my father's confidentiality, Dr. Bradley."

"Not when it's a common condition that will eventually be impossible to conceal, no. Judge Hathaway has cataracts growing on both eyes. Unusual for both eyes to be effected simultaneously, but not unheard of. I referred him to a specialist at the hospital in Danville. Let's see, how long ago was it?" Once more he swiveled away, apparently his favorite thinking position, then swiveled back. "Two months, I believe. He probably still has some vision left. There's no telling how long the progression will take since cataracts are notorious for growing at their own pace. He should have told you, but since he didn't, I will. The Judge will go completely blind before an operation is possible. But don't worry. Nowadays cataract removal is almost one hundred percent successful."

Susannah felt stunned. The Judge, going blind? How horrible! And no wonder that although he always had a book in hand, as was his lifelong habit, he never seemed to be reading those books. "I'm glad you told me," she said honestly, rising from her chair, "and I apologize if I was too, ah, pushy about my mother. I appreciate your time, and of course you'll bill me for it."

"I'll do no such thing!" Dr. Bradley smiled broadly, which had a nice softening effect on his thin face. He came out from behind his desk.

"If you insist." Susannah also smiled. She hadn't liked the man, but the pleasant expression made her think that she'd probably judged prematurely. "Anyway, thank you."

He followed as she went back to the waiting room to retrieve her coat. "Will you be staying in Kinloch long, Ms. Hathaway?"

"I'm not sure," she replied, allowing him to hold the coat as she slipped her arms into it. As she did so she thought about her father's impending blindness, and in that moment made a decision she'd been tending toward for days. "I'll certainly stay to see the Judge through his surgery, however long that takes. And there's the restoration of Laird's Mount—I want to continue my mother's work there. You see, she left the property to me."

The doctor's pale eyes widened. "I'm delighted, on both counts. In that case, Ms. Hathaway—I wonder if I may call you Susannah?" She nodded, and he continued, "I'd like it very much, Susannah, if you would be my guest for dinner some evening. Both the country club and the Inverness Inn have excellent food, as good as in any big city."

"Well, I, uh—" she hesitated, then thought, *Why the heck not?* "I'd enjoy that, Doctor. Sometime after Christmas."

"Don't think of me as a doctor, think of me as a friend. Unless, of course, you get sick, and we'll hope that doesn't happen. My name is Marvin."

"Marvin." Susannah smiled back over her shoulder as she went out the door.

"I'll be in touch, Susannah," he promised.

SUSANNAH SAID into the telephone, "Tomorrow night? You mean Christmas Eve?" She ran a hand through her hair—this was unexpected. "Well, yes, I guess I could. But—" she stopped herself. If Paul Starbuck chose to have dinner with her on Christmas Eve, who was she to ask why he wouldn't prefer to spend it with friends or family? She laughed softly as she listened to him effectively counter her "but."

"Enough! You've talked me into it. Tell me where and what time, and I'll meet you there."

She listened again and planted a hand on her hip— maybe this was a mistake—she hadn't meant to make a date with Mr. Macho. With exaggerated patience Susannah said, "No, Paul, I'm not too proud to ride in your truck. You have a magnificent-looking truck." She paused to listen to him "I am *not* being sarcastic. I have this policy. The first time I go out with some-body—*anybody*—I prefer to have my own wheels.

That's just the way I am, it has nothing to do specifically with you. Policy's policy. Take it or leave it."

He took it, specifying the Inverness Inn at seventhirty. There was something about the man that made Susannah want to have the last word, so she said, "Actually, there was something I wanted to talk to you about, anyway. I was going to call you, but now it can wait until tomorrow night."

She hung up with a small smile of satisfaction. Later she realized that he'd made her smile, and even laugh a little. Something no other man had done in a long time, even before her mother's death had turned her life upside down.

SUSANNAH FELT A PANG of regret as she looked at herself in the full-length mirror on the back of the bedroom door. The dress was new, and when she'd tried it on in a store in Boston, she'd looked into the mirror—just as she was doing now—and had thought, *Mother would like this dress.* It was amber velvet, simply yet cleverly cut with a slight flare to the skirt. The color, which brought out gold glints in her dark blond hair, had attracted Susannah, and her mother would have especially liked the wide collar of ecru lace.

Susannah smoothed the collar, wondering if she should take the time to snip a few threads and remove it now that Jane was no longer here to please. Her mother had been the one who liked ribbons and lace, and it had taken most of Susannah's adolescent years to convince her mother that the frills that looked so delightful on a tiny woman didn't do the same thing for her tall, long-boned daughter.

No, she decided, she would keep the collar and wear the dress tonight for Christmas Eve. But she'd wear it for Paul Starbuck, not for her mother. Tonight she would not be putting the gifts she'd bought under the tree. There was no tree, and she had left the gifts in a closet in Cambridge. She'd selected them with extra care and gone to unusual expense, to make up for the fact that the previous Christmas she hadn't joined her mother and the Judge in their new home; she'd gone skiing with friends, instead. More guilt. Maybe Paul Starbuck would help relieve that guilt.

For the Judge, Susannah had chosen an antique map of Virginia in the seventeenth century—she could see it in her mind's eye and remembered how she'd debated whether or not to frame it. In the end, to make it easier to carry on the plane, she'd left the map rolled up in the tube the shop had given her for it.

I should have brought the map with me, for the Judge, Susannah thought . . . and suddenly she was overwhelmed with sadness. She looked once more into the mirror, hating herself for bringing the new dress and not the Judge's gift. She should be in proper mourning, wearing black.

"I shouldn't be going out with Paul," Susannah said, stepping back from the mirror and sinking down on the side of the bed. "I should stay here with the Judge. He needs me, whether he thinks so or not."

*He may need you, but he doesn't want you here,* said the little voice inside her head that told her such things. Susannah put her hands over her face and tried fiercely not to cry.

HALF AN HOUR LATER, dry-eyed and with a tremulous smile pasted on her lips, Susannah approached a table in the small dining room of the Inverness Inn. Paul Starbuck's face lit up when he saw her, and in response, Susannah's smile gained firmer hold.

Seeing his huge frame tamed by suit, collar and tie, she thought to herself, *Hey, you clean up real good.* She greeted him confidently. "Hi, Paul."

"Hi. You look great, Susannah." He stood politely as the maitre d' pulled out her chair.

"I almost canceled out on you," Susannah confessed as she opened the menu. "At the last minute I felt I shouldn't leave the Judge."

"Oh. I'm sorry, I didn't think of that. I only thought about it being a sad kind of Christmas for you, and I was alone, so..." He didn't have to complete the apology with words, his eyes did it for him. He had beautiful, expressive eyes; black-lashed, a deep sapphire blue.

"Don't be sorry. My father prefers to handle his grief by being alone, and I don't seem to be quite sure how to handle mine." She tossed her head slightly to flip the hair back from her face. "I guess I can handle it best by getting on with my life. Though it's going to be a different kind of life. At least, for a while. Now, what's good here?"

Paul surprised her—she would have guessed him to be a strict meat-and-potatoes man, but he wasn't. He discussed the sophisticated menu so knowledgeably that Susannah decided to let him order for her. When he'd done so, she said, "I don't mean to pry, but how do you happen to be alone at this family-oriented time of year?"

He flashed an impish grin. "I'd like to get your sympathy by telling you there's just me and Wolf, but that's not exactly the truth."

"Wolf?" Susannah raised her eyebrows.

"Yeah. I had her with me the other day but I left her in the truck. She's home now, protecting the house from bad guys, or the Grinch, or whoever. Wolf is a great watchdog."

"Let me get this straight. You have a wolf for a companion and watchdog?"

The impish grin widened. "She's part German Shepherd. Who knows what the other part is? Could be wolf. She looks it, so that's what I call her. Smartest dog in the South."

"I see." Susannah hadn't had much experience with animals. Pets hadn't been allowed when she was growing up.

"Your mother didn't like Wolf. Well, actually, Jane was afraid of her. Seems she'd been attacked by a big dog when she was a child and had a fear of them ever since. But why am I telling you? You'd know that. Anyway, I got in the habit of leaving Wolf at home or in the truck whenever I'd go to Laird's Mount—that's why you didn't see her with me the other day."

Susannah hadn't known about her mother's fear of dogs. Yet Paul knew. And Dr. Marvin Bradley knew something about Jane that he wasn't telling. Susannah began to wonder how many things about her mother she hadn't known, or didn't know.

"Penny for them," said Paul.

"What?" Susannah blinked and widened her eyes.

"Your thoughts." He waved a fork. "I'm over here, remember? Big guy in the fancy duds. You were a million miles away."

He spoke with just the right humorous touch to bring her back from thoughts that were making her uncomfortable. She appreciated that. Susannah smiled and asked him a question she'd wondered when they were introduced. "Your surname is very...distinctive. What's the origin of Starbuck? Sounds a little Indian. Excuse me, I mean Native American."

"You don't have to be politically correct with me, I'm just an old country boy. Anyway, I don't know about roots and all that, but the Starbucks have been in Maine for a lot of generations. I come from a big family. I could have gone home for the holidays, but sometimes all those relatives are too much for me. I'm the only one down here in Virginia."

"And what brought you here?"

"Work. And money. I started out to be an architect, like you, but—well, something happened. A family thing, and I couldn't finish school."

Susannah put down her fork. There had been a glint of something dark in Paul's eyes, and a barely perceptible tightening of his lips, but now it was gone. She said, "I'm sorry. But surely you could go back and finish if you wanted to? There are loans and things, and Virginia Tech in Blacksburg is a fine school—''

"Nah!" Finished with his meal, Paul leaned back in his chair. "After a while I realized that I'd rather work with my hands—I'm better with my hands than I am with my head, anyway. So I became a contractor, and pretty soon I'd decided to specialize in restoration. I'm more interested in preserving good old architecture than I am in building something new. And to tell the truth, I kind of like getting dirty. It's more fun that way."

He's like an overgrown kid, Susannah thought, thoroughly enjoying his company.

"Anyhow, that's how I got here. From Virginia down through the Carolinas there's more interesting old architecture per square mile than just about anywhere else in the country, and a lot of it's like here in Kinloch, just waiting for somebody with money to come along and care. They're coming. Retirees, like your mother and father, seeking out the small Southern towns mostly because of the warmer climate, wanting the slower pace. Now Jane, her interest was a really good example of the kind of thing that can happen."

"Oh? How so?"

Paul leaned forward and pushed his plate aside to make room for his elbows, in his enthusiasm forgetting his manners. "Some people when they retire, they just kind of close up or play a lot of golf or something. Others, they find new interests and get really involved. That's what she was doing. Didn't she tell you?''

"No, not exactly. She told me about buying Laird's Mount, but she didn't say much." Susannah wrinkled her brow, trying to remember. "I got the impression that what Mother really wanted was to show me a lot of things, and I thought that would happen on this Christmas visit I'd planned. I was going to stay the week from Christmas to New Year's. And now—well, you know. Go on, tell me more."

"Okay. Kinloch has a group of people interested in historic preservation, and Jane got involved in that right away after moving here, which is how she heard about Laird's Mount. I gather the Judge—well, he had his own interests. Nobody saw much of him, but Jane was all over the place. People took to her—she was easy to like. Next thing you know she'd bought Laird's Mount. It was quite a coup, hadn't even gone on the market. I guess her buying the place put some people's noses out of joint, but that's a whole other subject."

"Oh! Somebody else said that to me, very recently. It was the doctor, Marvin Bradley. I went to see him, and he mentioned that he'd wanted to buy the place himself."

"Well, thank the good Lord Jane got to it first! I'd hate to have to be working with him instead of her!" He leaned back again, running his hand through his black hair. "Jeez, listen to me. I'm sorry. I guess it hasn't really sunk in that she's gone."

"I know what you mean. It was just so sudden."

"Yeah. And such a damn shame it had to happen when she was making a whole new life for herself."

Susannah tensed. "What do you mean, a whole new life?"

"Oh, God, if you didn't know then maybe I shouldn't be telling you this. But I'm sure Jane would have told you herself. She must have been saving it for this visit of yours. She was so excited about restoration! Jane did a lot of work, a lot of painstaking research before we touched so much as a single brick on Laird's Mount. She loved it, had a natural talent for it, an instinct. Her plan was to restore the house and then sell it, then buy another and restore it and sell it, and so on. She looked on the work at Laird's Mount as the beginning of a career, and that was why she was so excited. She'd never had a career. She could have done it, she was still young enough and she certainly was smart enough. I was going to help her."

"I see," said Susannah. Her head was spinning. Jane, with a career? What had the Judge thought about that? How had he felt about Jane being involved with something that took her away from him for hours at a time? Paul might know, but Susannah wasn't going to ask—that was too big a can of worms to open at present. And maybe it didn't matter anymore.

She said, "Paul, when you asked me out I said I had something to tell you. Remember?"

He nodded, lips curved in a restrained grin. "I remember. I was curious as hell, and you just left me hanging."

"I won't keep you hanging any longer. I've decided to stay in Kinloch. I'll have to go back to Cambridge and close up my apartment, but that shouldn't take more than a few days. I'm also going to resign from the firm I've been working with—I haven't liked the kind of things they had me doing, I was getting frustrated, and it was time for a change, anyway."

"That's a pretty big step. You sure you want to resign? I mean, it's none of my business, but right after a death in the family may not be the best time for making big decisions."

Susannah nailed him with a steely glance. She liked the guy, but he could get out of line pretty fast. "You're right, it isn't any of your business. Except, in a way it could be. There are a couple of reasons for my staying here. One of them is Laird's Mount. I've decided to complete the work my mother began. I presume you'll continue on as contractor? I want you to. I'm not sure I could do it without you."

Paul scowled darkly. He took his time before answering. "Well, I've been wondering about that, of course. I don't usually work with architects, there aren't that many who specialize in restoration. And the ones that do, they have an attitude—" He stopped abruptly and looked into her eyes.

Susannah said quietly, "Well, there will be a lot for me to learn." She held his look for what seemed like ages. She saw his eyes grow darker.

At that moment the waiter appeared with the check. Paul seized it, glanced at it and plunked his money down on the table. "Let's get out of here. We'll finish talking on the way home."

Mutely, wondering about *his* attitude, Susannah followed as Paul ungraciously preceded her to the door. He went on through while she stopped to get her coat from the cloakroom. When she stepped out onto the Inn's porch into the brisk winter air, he was waiting. "We came separately," she reminded him, "so we can't finish talking on the way home. I guess we can do it right here."

"Yeah. Look, Susannah, I'd like to work out a deal. I'll buy Laird's Mount from you. As is. It would take me a while to pay, but—hell, you don't seem to need the money, and I could keep on with the restoration a little at a time. Pay you whatever balance I owe when I'm finished and sell the place. What do you say?"

"What's this all about, Paul? You don't want to work with me just because I'm an architect? Not only that, I'm a *female* architect? Because if that's what's bugging you, I can tell you I've had it with that sort of thing up to here!" She threw one hand in the air over her head. A gust of wind picked up the ends of her hair and left her neck exposed to the cold. In her growing anger, she didn't feel it.

Paul shoved his hands in his pockets, looked at Susannah, and his eyes softened. "It's cold out here. Let's talk in the truck."

"No. I don't think we have all that much more to say to each other." Susannah glanced around and saw four porch rockers. "We can sit over there. It's not that cold."

"If you weren't so damn independent or whatever, we could be warm right now," grumbled Paul as he joined her. "Look, Susannah, I made you a serious proposition. You should think it over. You don't have to give me an answer now."

"And I asked you a serious question, which I *do* expect you to answer now."

"You mean about me not wanting to work with you because you're a woman architect?" Susannah nodded. He said, "It's not that. At least, not the woman part—women have as much right to be architects as anybody else lucky enough to afford all those years of school, getting started in practice..."

"You have a chip on your shoulder, after all. I thought you liked working with your hands, getting dirty and all that."

Paul shot her a murderous glance. He said, "All right. You have a chip on your shoulder, too, but I'll ignore it. Where I'm coming from is, I just never anticipated any of this. *A,* that Jane would die, *b,* that she'd leave you the house—"

"And all her money," said Susannah grimly, since money seemed to be such an important consideration for him.

He responded to her interruption in a voice that was low, tense and tightly controlled. "You really know how to rub it in, don't you, Susannah?"

"I'm just being practical."

"To continue, *c,* I never thought you'd want to take on the restoration yourself. Ever since the other day when I saw you out there, I've been thinking and thinking about how I could work it to buy the house from you."

"Well, we can put an end to this debate very quickly. I'm not going to sell Laird's Mount. I am going to restore it, and when it's done I may or may not sell. Who knows, I may decide to live there myself. Now, are you going to work with me on this, or not?"

"I have to think about it. I'll let you know."

They went their separate ways. Susannah was halfway home before she realized she'd forgotten to thank him for the dinner.

# Chapter Three

"Wolf, old girl, old friend, you're gonna have to help me out on this." Paul Starbuck was talking to his dog.

Recognizing her name and the tone of her master's voice, Wolf pushed her slightly shaggy black-and-silver self up into a sitting position. She was in her favorite spot—the center of the oval braided rug on Paul's living room floor. Wolf cocked her head and looked at him with bright, intelligent yellow eyes.

Paul was also in his favorite spot, a battered easy chair that he'd been meaning to get reupholstered for at least three years. Nothing in the room matched, yet it somehow went together in a comfortable way, like an old crazy quilt. He smiled and said, "Yeah, that's right. Pay attention."

"Woof!" said Wolf, panting in a friendly fashion.

"There's this woman named Susannah. Wait till you see her, she's all class. Tall—I mean *really* tall—and lean, moves like some sort of athlete, but she sure doesn't look like any athlete I've ever seen. She has such grace, it gives her a kind of—I don't know—dignity. She looks like some kind of goddess...."

Paul fell silent and forgot about his dog as he mused over Susannah. As long as he lived he'd never forget how she looked when she walked toward him at the Inn, wearing the most perfect dress he'd ever seen, made out of a fabric that had depth and texture to it, that gleamed golden when she moved, and emphasized the gold lights in her hair. You wouldn't say she was gorgeous, she was more than that. He'd never known anyone who could touch Susannah with a ten-foot pole, for looks or brains, or anything else.

Wolf padded across the rug and put her head in Paul's lap. He absently scratched her behind an ear. "That's the trouble, old girl. She's too good for me, it's a fact. She has *everything*—including Laird's Mount and a degree in architecture."

Yeah, Susannah had everything, but it was clear she wasn't happy. Paul was pretty sure there was more to her unhappiness than her mother's death. Sometimes, in the two short chunks of time he'd spent with Susannah, he'd felt as if there was a little girl somewhere inside that woman's body—and that little girl was hurting. When she got on her high horse she was just protecting herself.

"Woof!" said Wolf loudly. She sat and put a large paw on Paul's knee.

"Oh, so you think I deserved being put in my place, do you? Well maybe I did. The real question is, can I work with her? I just don't know."

Wolf smiled broadly, opening her mouth to show her pink tongue. She dipped her head, down-up, down-up.

Paul grinned. "I swear to God, Wolf, sometimes I think you really do understand everything I say. Yeah, I want to do it, but it'll be a hell of a lot different from working with Jane. I felt real affection for Jane, admired her, too. She had spunk. But Susannah—" He ran his hand through his too-curly hair the way he always did when he was thinking something he wasn't sure he should say. In this case, he wasn't sure he should even think it.

Paul confessed to Wolf, "The real trouble is that I'm so damn attracted to her. Physically attracted. And that's a dangerous mix, old girl, to be physically attracted to somebody you're gonna have to work closely with. Have to see her day after day, not dare to touch her..." Susannah wouldn't want him to touch her. Would she?

Paul got extremely uncomfortable wondering what the answer to that question might be. He switched his thoughts to the late Jane Hathaway, instead. Wolf, deciding that her opinions were no longer needed, lay down next to his chair, put her head on her paws and went to sleep.

What had happened to Jane was a mystery. Jane herself had been a kind of mystery. The nature of the relationship between Jane and the Judge and Susannah was also hard for Paul to understand. He came from a large, happy, close-knit family. He couldn't even begin to imagine doing what Susannah had done—let a couple of years go by between visits. Obviously there'd been emotional as well as physical distance between the parents and the daughter. Why was that? Who or what caused the distance?

Yet, in spite of that distance, Susannah had picked up right away that there was something strange about the way her mother had died. Not only picked up on it, but had seemed determined to pursue it. What could she do? What could anybody do?

Jane was not what she seemed. Her facade was a hell of a lot thicker than his own, but it was still a facade, that of the utterly devoted wife and society matron, full of social graces. Underneath, Jane Hathaway had been smart in the same way city kids are street smart. You might say cunning. You should definitely say manipulative. In the sweetest possible way, but still manipulative. She'd smile that knockout smile, listen to you with that utterly charming expression on her heart-shaped face, and have you wrapped around her little finger in a second.

Paul moved in and out of the social circles that the Judge and Jane had immediately entered on coming to Kinloch. You might say he worked both sides of the road, the white-collar side and the blue-collar side, and he was equally comfortable in both. He'd been to plenty of parties where both Hathaways were present, and to some where Jane had come alone—especially in recent months. He'd seen how Jane gravitated toward the men, how she charmed them. The Judge seemed like a devoted husband, a distinguished old man who somehow had never quite gotten over his awe of his much younger, very beautiful wife. Jane had been beautiful, all right. And she had looked a good ten years younger than she really was.

Paul had admitted to himself a long time ago that he wasn't immune to Jane's charms. Of course, at thirty-eight, he was young enough to have been her son, but still... There was the one time she'd been within an inch of coming on to him. They'd necessarily spent a lot of time alone together at Laird's Mount. Their mutual pleasure in the early stages of the restoration, the discoveries they'd made together—of things like the ghost marks on the bricks that showed where the original porch had been—had naturally brought them close. And one day, about a year ago— God, he'd never forget it!

Paul stirred in his chair and ran a hand hastily through his hair. Jane had asked his age, and he'd told her. She'd remarked, with her bright blue eyes just inches from his face, that there was precisely the same difference in age between herself and the Judge, but in the opposite direction. Then she'd cocked her head, and the tip of her tongue had come out to delicately touch her upper lip, and she'd said women were so much smarter nowadays. Paul had been aware there was something going on here, but he'd taken the bait. He'd asked, How do you mean? And Jane had said, *It's perfectly acceptable now for a woman to have a younger lover. It makes good sense, if you think about it, since women live so much longer than men. In my case, with the Judge being almost eighty, I'll be alone before long and I have to be realistic. I have to be ready for the future.*

Nothing had come of it, of course. Nothing except a little thread of desire that ran between him and an older, still-beautiful woman. He'd felt it, but he'd broken that thread. If he hadn't . . .

Paul felt disloyal in the memory. Jane had been trying her wings, that was all. Maybe with men, certainly with the work she'd intended to make into a career. But he had to acknowledge, now that he really thought about it, that Jane Hathaway might have been considered a troublemaker by some people. It was possible that one of those people might have considered her enough trouble to want her dead.

How anyone could have killed her and made it look like a death from natural causes—well, that was another question, and Paul had done enough thinking for one night.

He stood up, stretched and yawned mightily. Wolf raised her head and thumped her tail once on the floor. "Yeah, I know, you want to go out."

"Woof!" Thump, thump. But Wolf wasn't ready to go out yet. She stayed where she was and looked up expectantly.

"Okay, so you want to know what I've decided, do you? Well, I think I'll leave Susannah alone for a few days. Who knows, maybe she'll change her mind and sell Laird's Mount to me, after all. If she doesn't, then I'll call and tell her that I'll work with her. Satisfied?"

Wolf grinned, got up, ambled over to the door and answered, "Woof."

Paul opened the door and watched his wolfish companion bound out into the night.

SUSANNAH'S FEW DAYS in Cambridge stretched to three weeks. As soon as she set foot in her apartment she realized that she hadn't thought things through very well. She couldn't just call up her boss, say, "I quit," lock her doors and walk out. Nothing was that simple. Her sense of Yankee thrift got in the way. She decided to sublet the apartment rather than let it remain empty, so she had to find a tenant. She had to sort through her things before packing up what possessions she would send on to Kinloch. There were details to be finished at work before she could turn over her current job, the design of a shopping center, to another of the firm's architects. And so on.

With the delays, Susannah was glad that before leaving Kinloch she'd acted over her father's objections and hired a couple, Tom and Sarah Parrish, to come in on a daily basis to cook and clean for the Judge and look after the yard. She had also told her father, without mentioning that she knew of his failing eyesight, that Tom Parrish was an experienced chauffeur. She hoped the Judge wouldn't try to drive if he couldn't see well enough to do it.

Susannah was also glad that she'd talked Paul Starbuck into staying on the job at Laird's Mount. He would be making progress in her absence, and she was eager to get back and see what he'd done and to learn what more there was to do.

Finally, all that remained of her life in Cambridge was the old Volvo. She didn't really need it anymore and was ready to sell it, but that proved unexpectedly hard to do. It felt so final, like burning bridges. She dithered, and she drove around and around familiar streets until eventually she realized that she was saying goodbye.

*But that's ridiculous!* Susannah thought. *I'll do what I have to do in Kinloch, be there a few months, and then I'll come back to Cambridge.* Her subconscious mind, however, seemed to know differently. She finished her silent goodbyes and then was able to sell the Volvo without a qualm. Susannah flew back to Kinloch the third week of January.

Tom Parrish, driving the Judge's black Lincoln, met her at the airport in Danville, the nearest city to Kinloch. The Judge was not with him, and Susannah felt a pang of disappointment that she knew was unreasonable. Just because she'd missed her father and worried about him was no reason for him to feel the same about her.

"I'll sit up front with you, Tom," she said, opening the car door for herself.

Tom Parrish looked doubtful, as if she were committing some breach of etiquette, but Susannah didn't care. He said, "Yes, ma'am" as he closed the door after her and went around to get into the driver's seat. He and his wife were African-American, and in their fifties. He was as short and fat as his wife was tall and thin—which Susannah had thought ironic since Sarah was the cook. But both were good-natured, and Tom smiled pleasantly as he got behind the wheel.

"How is my father?" Susannah asked when they were clear of the airport traffic.

"About the same. No better, no worse," said Tom.

It was the answer she'd expected. "I hope he hasn't tried to drive, that he's asked you to drive him wherever he wants to go."

"The Judge ain't been out of the house. First time he ever said anything 'bout drivin' was when he told me to come and get you, Miss Susannah."

She turned her head and looked at Tom. "Now that I'm back, I want us to get something straight, Tom. I don't like to be called ma'am, or Miss Susannah. And I certainly don't want you to call me Miss Hathaway, I'm not that formal a person. If I can call you Tom and your wife Sarah, then you can call me Susannah. All right?"

Tom smiled broadly. "All right. You're the boss."

"Good. And tell Sarah that's what I said, okay?"

"Okay, I'll tell her."

That accomplished, Susannah relaxed and looked out the car window. The countryside was beautiful, gently rolling, lightly dusted with snow. Cambridge and Boston had been clogged and rutted with old snow turned to ice. She sighed, enjoying the difference. Occasional trees, graceful in their winter nakedness, dotted the landscape.

"I'm glad to be back," said Susannah, and she thought, *This place is my home now—at least, for a while.* She could hardly wait to settle in and see for herself how the Judge was doing. And then she could call Paul Starbuck and really get going on Laird's Mount.

SUSANNAH HAD NOT DREAMED about her mother since before Christmas, but now the dream returned. It began in the way of the old dream, with Jane's face looming large in Susannah's mind. But then her mother's face receded and her own perspective changed. Susannah looked down on the interior of Laird's Mount as if from a great height. She saw Jane moving through the empty rooms, gliding like a ghost, trailing a small white hand along the stair banister. Again the dream shifted, Jane disappeared, and Susannah was alone inside the old house. She went from room to room as her mother had done, feeling dwarfed by the high ceilings, squinting in the gray gloom. On and on she went, through door after door, seeking a way out . . . and unable to find it. Someone was after her, someone was pursuing her, and she couldn't get away. She was trapped, trapped . . . !

With a great effort, Susannah tore herself out of the dream. Her eyes flew open on total darkness. For long moments she was still lost in dream panic, her heart thudding loud in her ears. She dug her fingers into the mattress, grasping for something—anything—to hold on to. She was frozen with fear, afraid to turn her head, afraid of what she might see if she dared look. Finally, she glanced to her left and saw the red numbers displayed on the bedside clock. The breath she'd been holding rushed out of her in a whoosh. She knew where she was: in the guest bedroom she'd claimed for her own in her father's house in Kinloch. Susannah turned on her side, pulled the covers up over her ears and whispered to herself, "It's all right, it was only a dream, only a dream . . ." Over and over, until at last she fell asleep again. But the fear was still with her when she next awoke, to daylight. The clock told her it was 8:00 a.m., a good hour later than she usually got up. Her heart fluttered, her hands felt cold and clammy.

*I need to run,* Susannah thought. She chased the cobwebs of fear from her mind as she hastily pulled on a navy blue sweat suit and heavy socks, and tied her running shoes. In the bath adjoining her room she splashed cold water on her face and tugged a headband down almost to her eyebrows. In her eagerness to be on her way, she skipped her warm-up stretches.

The outside air was gloriously crisp and clean. There were no sidewalks, though, and she didn't like to run across people's lawns. She settled for the side of the pavement, facing oncoming traffic, and kept to a slow jog at first. In minutes Susannah was feeling one-hundred-percent better. She'd been foolish to let all the recent disruption in her life take away her daily run— she wouldn't do that anymore.

Her father's street was soon behind her, and Susannah, jogging along, had a decision to make. Should she loop around back up a side street and explore other areas in her new neighborhood, or take the road that led to downtown Kinloch? She opted for the road, then looked left and right and jogged across, keeping to the side of the pavement as before. She lengthened her stride, puffing, feeling her lungs expand. All her muscles were loose now, and she was beginning to feel a glow inside. An occasional car or truck passed, drivers waved, and Susannah waved back. She felt on top of the world. She began to tire just at the edge of the downtown, but she pushed on.

There were sidewalks now, and small, well-tended buildings that she had paid scarce attention to before. In a pale gold wash of morning sun, Kinloch had a quiet, self-contained beauty. *I could learn to love it here,* she thought.

A runner's high gripped Susannah as she circled the block containing the town library, a Greek Revival, temple-style building surrounded by bright green, winter rye grass lawns in the very center of the downtown. She threw back her head, exulting, and flung out her arms. She felt like she was flying and did not notice the faces that looked out of windows, the figures that paused in doorways. They were watching an unusual sight in a rural Virginia town: a woman with streaming honey gold hair and very long legs and joy on her face, a woman who ran like the wind. Those who did not already know Susannah Hathaway by sight would soon make it their business to learn her name.

SUSANNAH'S CALL to Paul Starbuck was picked up by his answering service. "Out of town?" asked Susannah, barely able to hide her disappointment. "For how long? Oh. No, no message. I'll catch up with him when he returns."

She hung up and glared at the telephone. Three days! She tossed her head impatiently. Now she wished she'd kept in touch with Paul by telephone while she was in Cambridge—she didn't even know what stage the work was in. All she knew was that Paul had said he'd get the men started to work again and bring her up to date when she returned. Well, she was no stranger to construction sites, she could go out and take a look for herself.

But as Susannah put on her coat and reached for her purse and car keys, she went cold all over. She stood stock still, feeling again the fear with which she'd awakened that morning, remembering the dream of herself trapped in the old house. What if there was no one working there today? She didn't want to be there alone. Not today. Not yet.

There were other things she had to do. Laird's Mount could wait until she could go there with Paul for company. Susannah decided that she would go into town, instead. She needed to open an account at the bank. Perhaps she could persuade the Judge to come with her, and they could have lunch at that interesting little restaurant she'd noticed this morning on her run. She went to look for him.

The Judge was not in his study, nor was he in the kitchen, but Sarah Parrish was. She looked up from the kitchen counter where she was chopping celery; the kitchen was warm, its air moist and fragrant.

"Hi, Sarah," said Susannah, "whatever that is you're cooking, it smells great."

"It's just plain old vegetable soup, Susannah. Can I fix you some lunch?" she asked with a smile.

Susannah wished she had the Parrish's secret for appearing to be so contented all the time. "No, thank you. I was looking for my father. Do you know where he is?"

"Mos' likely he's in that study of his, sittin' with a book."

"I looked there, and he isn't. He didn't have Tom drive him anywhere?"

"No, ma'am. Susannah. Such a pretty name you have. You know that ol' song 'Oh, Susannah'?"

"Do I ever! When I was little the other kids used to tease me with that song."

"Nobody never call you Sue, for short?"

"No," Susannah said with a grin, "maybe because I've never been exactly short! Anyway, I'll keep looking for my father. Maybe he's in his room."

The Judge was indeed in his room, lying fully clothed on his bed with his hands clasped over his flat stomach. Susannah tiptoed in and noticed that he had removed his shoes. They were sitting neatly side by side on the floor near the bed. The Judge's eyes were closed, and his chest rose and fell regularly with his breathing. So he was okay, just sleeping. She left as quietly as she'd come, closing the door carefully to just a crack behind her.

He's depressed, Susannah thought as she drove away in her mother's white Honda Prelude, which was now her car. Seeing the Judge asleep before noon on a sunny winter day disturbed her, but she didn't know what she could do about it. Should she talk to Dr. Bradley? Was there a psychiatrist anywhere around Kinloch? Not that Judge Harold Hathaway could ever be forced to see a psychiatrist, anyway.

Friends, then—surely he must have made some friends in two years. Yet none had come to call after the post-funeral flurry of casserole-bearing females. There had been, as well as she could remember, a lot of people at the funeral, but they must have been there for Jane. Jane had been the social one, the one who reached out to people. The Judge was just too forbidding.

Susannah parked on the main street and tried to put her father's problems out of her mind. She checked inside the briefcase-size leather bag that she used for a purse—yes, all the papers she would need were there. She hoisted the strap onto her shoulder and climbed out. A rather tricky maneuver for a long-legged woman exiting a small car—her skirt rode up to mid-thigh in the process and she tugged it down absently as she checked to be sure she'd left the door locked.

"You don't have to do that here, you know," said a man's voice.

Susannah straightened up and turned around. "No, I suppose not, but old ways die hard. I'm just used to locking my car."

The man looked familiar, another one of those faces without names, from the funeral. He was a couple of inches shorter than she, had salt-and-pepper hair so curly that it looked permed, and a beefy face and broad body. A businessman, to judge from the way he was dressed. He said, "I don't expect you to remember—"

Susannah interrupted him. She was coming to hate those words, and if they were inevitable she would rather say them herself. "Yes, we met at my mother's funeral. I'm Susannah Hathaway, which I guess you knew, but I'll have to ask your name. I'm afraid I met so many people, and the whole thing was like one big blur in my mind."

"Charles Herbert. May I call you Susannah?"

Because of the way his eyes roamed her body and lingered on her legs, which no doubt he'd gotten a good gander at when her skirt rode up, Susannah felt like saying, No, you certainly may not! But she squared her shoulders, tossed her hair back out of her eyes and said, "Of course. I'm just on my way to the bank, Mr. Herbert." And she started walking to the bank, which was halfway up the block.

"Charles. I'm going there myself, so I'll just walk along with you."

Susannah gritted her teeth and thought, *Just my luck!* For some reason she took an instant dislike to this man. She didn't bother to reply, since he was already walking so close to her side that their arms brushed. She angled away and lengthened her stride.

"I'm the local Realtor. Oh, there are others, but I'm *the* one. Kinloch Realty, that's me. I was a great friend of your mother's."

"Were you?" Susannah regarded him from the corner of her eye. The fleshy face wore a smug expression. In spite of it, she had to admit that some women would think this man handsome—star high school football player grows up and becomes sucessful businessman.

"Yep. I was the one who put your mother on to Laird's Mount. Did her a real favor there, and she wasn't one to forget!"

*Oh, really?* He didn't wink, but he might as well have. "Then I suppose I should thank you," said Susannah, "since Laird's Mount is mine now."

Outside the bank door, he stopped. "I've been wanting to talk to you about that, but I heard you'd gone back to—where was that?"

"Cambridge. I'm not aware we have anything to talk about, Mr. Herbert." Susannah stood impatiently.

"Aw, come on now, Susannah, call me Charles, or Charlie. Lot of my friends call me Charlie, but not Jane, she had too much class. She called me Charles. What I want to talk about is Laird's Mount, of course, about when you plan to put the place back on the market. There are a lot of folks around here just itching to get hold of that place. I went up there the other day, just to see how the work is coming on. Starbuck's done a good bit already. You could turn a tidy profit right this very minute."

*I'm going to lock those gates,* thought Susannah. She smiled a falsely sweet smile. "I'm getting the idea, *Charles,* that Kinloch has a pretty efficient grapevine.

So I'm surprised you haven't heard the news. I don't intend to sell Laird's Mount. So you see, we have nothing to talk about." She reached out and pushed open the bank's door.

He jumped into action, pushing the door farther inward and putting himself in her path. He lowered his voice an octave, intimately. "You ought to talk to me. Really. You owe it to your mother. There are things about that old house that you don't know. Things I could tell you."

As obnoxious as he was, that got Susannah's attention. "All right, I give up, you got me. When and where?"

He took her elbow and pulled her aside, a few steps from the door. "Tell you what, I'll buy you lunch. Right now, after we finish our business here."

Really, the man was too much! Susannah shook her head. "Can't. I have another commitment." She didn't, but no way would she do anything even slightly social with him.

"Okay, then." He fished inside his jacket. "Here's my card. My office, two o'clock. Address is on there."

"I guess I can make that," agreed Susannah. She was intensely curious. What had he meant, that Jane wasn't one to forget favors? What could there be about Laird's Mount that she didn't know, and ought to know?

# Chapter Four

Susannah's bank business involved the kind of money that earned her discreetly preferential treatment. A teller ushered her into a glass-walled cubicle, where a female bank officer sat behind a large desk.

"Ms. Hathaway?" The woman rose and extended her hand, saying, "I'm Angelica Herbert."

Susannah shook hands. "How do you do."

"I'll be glad to assist you. If you will tell me exactly how you would like your accounts set up..."

Opening the large leather bag, Susannah brought out bankbooks and papers, her own from Cambridge and those that had come to her from the lawyers in the settlement of her mother's estate. She explained what she had in mind, and was soon filling out forms while she stole glances at Angelica Herbert.

The woman was relatively young, yet wore her dark hair in an old-fashioned way, parted in the center and waved down over her ears before disappearing into a bun at the back of her head. The severe style did no favors for her narrow face. She was handsomely dressed in a navy blue suit, she was also quick and efficient, but something in her manner put Susannah on guard. As she signed her name time after time, she worked out what it was: Angelica Herbert lacked the casual friendliness that Susannah had come to expect in Kinloch. In fact, she was borderline hostile.

"Will there be a waiting period," Susannah asked to break the cold silence, "or will my funds be available immediately?"

"Just a minute," said Angelica. Her long fingers were busy at the computer keyboard on her desk. She tap-tap-tapped and frowned at the computer screen— the frown was probably habitual, judging from the depth of the vertical line between her eyebrows.

Susannah suddenly wished that Kinloch had more than one bank. She didn't like having her finances scrutinized by this unfriendly woman.

Angelica shot Susannah a severe look, then turned away from the computer and, with difficulty, smoothed out the frown. "To answer your question, the transfer of your Cambridge account will take forty-eight hours to clear. However, I have just completed the in-house transfer of the money from your mother's formerly frozen checking account into the one you have opened. That amount is available to you now, today." She opened a drawer, took out a checkbook and wrote in it, then shoved it across the desk to Susannah. "These are your temporary checks. The imprinted ones will arrive in the mail in about two weeks. I see you are living at your father's address."

"Yes, I am." Susannah gathered up the checkbook and the legal papers and put them into her bag.

"You intend to stay permanently in Kinloch, Ms. Hathaway?" Angelica's expression was now one of avid curiosity. Her eyes, like her hair, were so dark they were almost black, and they glittered.

Susannah was equally curious. People did not usually react so coldly to her, not even in the supposedly less cordial north. She decided to try to evoke a little warmth. "My father is not exactly well, Mrs. Herbert. My mother's death was a terrible shock for him. He's not himself, so I'm staying with him indefinitely."

"Yes, Jane Hathaway's death was a shocking surprise for everyone." The dark eyes glittered even more brightly. "For those of us who knew her, I mean, and most people did."

Angelica did not offer the usual condolences, and while in a way Susannah was grateful for that, she also wondered why. "I suppose you knew my parents socially, as well as through bank business? I couldn't help but notice, Mrs. Herbert, that you have the same last name as a man I met coming into the bank, and he implied that he knew my mother well. Are you related to Charles Herbert, the Realtor?"

The glittering eyes shifted into a freezing stare. "Not anymore. Charles Herbert is my ex-husband. We are recently—very recently—divorced."

"Oh." Susannah threw caution to the winds and grinned. "Well, if first impressions are good for anything, I'd guess you're probably better off without him. Now, before I put any more of my foot in my mouth, I'd better be going."

Angelica thawed. A faint smile softened the severe lines of her face. "You didn't put your foot in your mouth, Ms. Hathaway. In fact, you couldn't have said anything more correct! But I suppose I should caution you not to make that kind of remark to most of the people you meet in this town. Charlie's pretty well liked. You asked earlier if I knew your parents socially. I didn't, not really. Since the separation, I haven't had much of a social life. If it weren't for my job, well—" She stopped short and shrugged, rather eloquently.

Susannah's heart went out to the woman. She suspected Angelica's air of hostility was some kind of a defense mechanism, probably directly related to the divorce. It didn't have anything to do with Susannah herself, at all. Without the frown she was much more approachable, and attractive, probably in Susannah's own age range. As Susannah stood to go, she said warmly, "Believe me, I can understand that. I haven't been in Kinloch long enough to make many friends. Perhaps, if you're at loose ends, we could get together sometime."

The barest beginning of a frown formed. "I don't know, I—"

"Well, think about it. Call if you're interested."

"All right, I will."

"I BET YOU MET MY WIFE at the bank," said Charles Herbert later that afternoon, leaning back comfortably in one of two upholstered chairs in his real estate office.

Susannah smiled with mock sweetness. "If you mean your ex-wife, yes, I did. She helped me get my accounts set up."

"I figured. New accounts are her department. She didn't waste any time telling you about the divorce, did she?" His attitude conveyed that he didn't mind a bit. Probably saved him having to tell her himself that he was available.

"I remarked on your having the same last name, and she set me straight. But I didn't come here to discuss your personal life, Charles. I'm interested in what you said earlier. That there were things about Laird's Mount that I should know."

"Yeah." He hitched up one trouser leg and set an ankle on the opposite knee. He smiled in a calculatedly charming way that revealed two dimples in his florid cheeks. "Spoke out of turn there. I expect I just wanted to be sure I'd get to see you again, Susannah."

Her own smile disappeared, replaced by a withering glance. "If I'd known this would be a waste of time—"

"Whoa, hold on a second! Anybody ever tell you you're skittish as a colt, Susannah? Since when is it a waste of time to be alone with a beautiful woman?"

"I was speaking of *my* time, Mr. Herbert. Not yours." Susannah tossed her head. She was tempted to leave immediately. The only reason she didn't was that she was still curious about what he had to say. "Now, either we can have a businesslike discussion and you can tell me what you originally intended to say, or I'll be on my way."

"Okay, okay." Charles put both feet on the floor and leaned forward, resting his elbows on thick thighs. "The thing is, that piece of property has a bad reputation. Your mother didn't know, I never told her, and after what happened to her...well, I felt kind of bad about not telling her. Not that there's any connection...but I thought I should tell you, that's all, before you go making any big plans."

"Piece of property—you mean Laird's Mount? What sort of bad reputation?"

He hesitated, then said, "It's supposed to be haunted."

Susannah looked at Charles Herbert in sheer disbelief. "You mean, there's a *ghost* at Laird's Mount?"

"Yeah. Listen, Susannah, not many people know about the ghost and I wouldn't want you spreading the word around. It wouldn't be in your best interest for when you go to sell the place. And you will want to sell it, like your mother did, just as soon as you finish the restoration. What I don't understand is, why not go ahead and let me put the house on the market now? I mean, before anything else happens. You could get your money out, and I'd get a nice commission. Believe me, that would be the best thing all around."

Every long Yankee bone in Susannah's body rebelled against what this ex-jock businessman was telling her in his soft Southern accent, with an oh-so-sincere look on his face. Believe him? Not a word of it! She reacted, speaking without thinking. "I don't believe in ghosts—that's just a lot of romantic nonsense. I thought maybe you knew something important or relevant. But a ghost? Honestly!''

"I think you're making a mistake. I think you should listen to me on this ghost business."

"What I think, Charles Herbert, is that where you're really coming from is the last word you said—*business*. And as I said before, you and I don't have any to conduct. Not only am I not going to sell Laird's Mount, I'm going to be living there myself, just as soon as the house is in good-enough shape for me to move in!'' She got up from her chair decisively, hoisting the large leather bag onto her shoulder.

"Oh, Lord," said Charles, rubbing a hand over his face as he also got to his feet. "Look, you misunderstand me. I shouldn't say this, but if I don't—''

"If you shouldn't say it—no matter what it is—then I'd rather you didn't. Goodbye, Mr. Herbert."

He said it, anyway, murmuring to himself as he looked out his office window to watch Susannah cross the street. "Your mama could've died of fright. Something killed that poor woman and didn't leave a mark on her. Could've been the ghost, Miss High-and-Mighty Hathaway!''

RETURNING FROM three days' consultation on a restoration across the state line in North Carolina, Paul Starbuck squinted at the declining sun and consulted his watch. His crew should be on the job at Laird's Mount for another half hour yet.

"Let's check in," he said to Wolf, who sat upright in the passenger seat of his truck, "see how they're doing."

"Woof," the dog agreed.

A few minutes later he passed through the brick pillars that supported the open iron gate. The dark red-brick of the house, upon the apex of its surrounding lands, gleamed a rosy cast from the late afternoon sunlight. Rather than drive on around to the parking area on the side, Paul stopped near the mounting block at the end of the walk. Wolf looked at him and panted expectantly.

"You can get out and run around while I'm inside. But don't go far—we won't be here long." He held the door, smiling, while Wolf left the truck in a graceful leap and took off across the wide brown lawn. Paul stretched to get rid of the driving kinks, and then started up the long walk to the front door of Laird's Mount. He didn't often go in this way, usually he entered from the rear of the side wing nearest the parking area. With his ever-assessing eye, Paul noted that the walkway needed a lot of work, many of the bricks were missing and still more were broken. But that was work that would be done by a landscape expert. Even with the walk in disrepair the approach to the house was still grand, marked by a double row of pecan and dogwood trees that were at least two hundred years old.

Paul stopped several feet short of the three steps up to the entry portico, his gaze roaming the whole facade. The months of work he'd done before Jane's death were not visible to the naked eye. They weren't supposed to be; that was the genius of this work, the most intricate he'd ever done on any restoration. And there was a new owner. Susannah. Could she appreciate what he'd been able to do? Would he even tell her? Paul sighed, running his hand through his hair. Yeah, he'd have to tell her—but whether or not she'd appreciate it was something else again. What if Susannah, the architect, thought his solution to a potentially terrible problem had been amateurish, or worse than that, wrong?

Paul stuck out his chin and began to climb the steps. He hadn't been wrong. What he'd done was brilliant, and he knew it. And anyway, maybe she wasn't even back in Kinloch yet. There was time to prepare himself for what he both wanted and dreaded—seeing Susannah Hathaway again.

Even before he opened the big, thick front door, Paul could hear sounds of work inside, of hammering and ripping. He knew what his crew was doing, so he took a deep breath and held it. He opened the door on a haze of plaster dust. He shouldn't stay in here long without a mask to protect his lungs.

Nobody heard Paul open the door. The men of his crew stood high above, balanced on a metal framework of scaffolding. They were tearing out the ceiling between the first and second floors, pulling down old plaster that had to be replaced, anyway, so that they could put in new utility lines and ductwork. They had to use the space between the ceilings and the floors above because all the walls in Laird's Mount, even the interior walls, were solid brick beneath their plastered and wood-paneled finish.

Paul stepped aside to avoid a crashing slab of plaster. He fished in his pocket and brought out a handkerchief to cover his nose and mouth. Then he looked up, assessing the progress his men had made. He was satisfied. That is, until he noticed that his four-man crew had grown to five. There was one too many. Someone he hadn't hired. A tall, skinny guy with a scarf on his head, up there on the far end of the scaffold. Who the hell was that?

Squinting against the foglike dust, Paul threaded his way through the lateral hall until he stood beneath the interloper. Like all the crew, the skinny guy was dressed in old jeans and a flannel work shirt covered in a whitish gray film of plaster dust. Like them, he wore a mask over his nose and mouth to avoid breathing in the dust. He was working just as hard as the rest of them, hammering cracked plaster loose with one hand and pulling it away from the wooden underlath with the other. But what kind of guy would put a paisley scarf on his head?

Under his breath, Paul muttered, "Oh, my God," and then he sneezed. He looked up again. That was no skinny guy, that was Susannah! Susannah Hathaway the architect, working right up there with his men!

His first impulse was to bellow out an order for her to get down from there. But you don't yell at somebody who's working fourteen feet up, you don't want to startle them. So Paul backed off and worked his way down the hall until he identified the short, square body of Tim, the foreman. He rapped on the metal pipe of the scaffolding to get Tim's attention, and when he had it, motioned him down and outside the front door.

Tim removed his mask, coughed once, took a deep breath of fresh air and asked, "Hey boss, what's happenin'? Didn't think we'd see you till tomorrow."

Paul shook out his handkerchief and stuck it back in his pocket. He ignored the foreman's question and asked his own. "What's *she* doing here?"

"She? Oh," Tim said with a grin, "you mean Susannah. She's workin' just like everybody else. She's pretty good, too. I had my doubts at first, but she keeps up just fine."

"You put her to work? Do you know who she is?"

"Yeah, sure. She came over here a couple of days ago, right about this time of day, and told us her name and that her mama had left her the house and all that. I walked around with her, showed her what we were doing. She asked a lot of questions and seemed to understand the answers, and then she said she wanted to help. Wanted to work alongside us a few hours a day. I didn't see any harm in it, but even if I had, what could I do? She's the *real* boss—I reckon if she wants to work, she can work."

"Yeah." Paul shoved his hands in his pockets. The real boss, huh? Jeez! He resisted, stubbornly. "But there's questions of safety, insurance, and all that."

"Oh, I watched her real close at first. She's careful. She won't get hurt. Leastways, no more'n the rest of us—you know, a few scratches and scrapes, a bruise now and then. She don't seem to mind. Susannah's a hell of an unusual woman."

Paul turned his head away. His jaw worked; he clenched and unclenched a fist. He felt as if his turf had been invaded, and he didn't like it. But there wasn't a damn thing he could do about it.

"Hey, Paul. What's the matter?" There was an edge of anxiety in Tim's voice.

"Nothing." Paul turned back. He didn't want to put Tim on the defensive. "But I'm going to get her to sign a release. Our insurance doesn't cover her, and I don't want Susannah to sue me if she falls off the scaffold and breaks her leg or something."

"I never thought of that. Listen, if I did wrong, I'm sorry."

Paul heaved a sigh. "You didn't do anything wrong. Listen, I don't want to go back in there until the dust settles. It's about quitting time, anyway. You go on and tell the men to knock off. Looks like you got a lot done while I was away. Good work, Tim."

"Thanks, boss."

Paul ambled on around the corner of the house to the side where everyone parked. He found a white Honda that looked like the car Jane used to drive, then leaned against the fender waiting for her to come out. Susannah was the last to appear—the others had left and he'd been about to go in after her when she finally stepped out onto the back porch and came down the steps.

She didn't see him. Paul's lips unconsciously curved in appreciation as she removed her scarf and shook out her hair. The setting sun gave it glints of rosy gold. She stretched out her arms and lifted her face so that it, too, was touched by the light. Then she bowed her head and rubbed the back of her neck.

Paul felt a stirring in his groin. God, she was beautiful! Dusty and dirty, but still beautiful. He ached with wanting to touch her, to rub her neck for her, and that hard-to-reach place between the shoulder blades...

Yet, as she began to walk toward her car, in the very moment when she looked straight at him and smiled, Paul's stubborn resistance returned. He moved away from the car, planted his feet wide apart and crossed his arms.

"I didn't know you were back," said Susannah, coming near. She was still smiling.

"Tim didn't tell you?"

"No, he didn't say anything. We thought you were due back in the morning."

"I got here a little early. Thought I'd come over and check out the progress."

Susannah rotated her shoulders, first one and then the other; she craned her neck back and forth. "Boy, am I going to be stiff tomorrow! But we got a lot done today. Would you like to come in and see?"

"I saw. I looked in for a couple of minutes before the guys knocked off and talked to Tim."

"Oh. I didn't see you."

"You were up on the scaffold. Surprised the hell out of me to see you up there. I didn't say anything because I didn't want to startle you."

Susannah rubbed at the back of her neck, staring at Paul with speculation in her gray eyes. He tried to make his face a mask; inside he was all conflicting emotions. On the one hand, he was sore at her for invading his turf, on the other hand, he just wanted to take her home with him and stand under a hot shower with her. Bits of white plaster clung to her hair like the finest snow. She had a smudge across one cheek where she'd rubbed it with a dirty hand. He wanted to wash her hair, soap her body and rub away its aches with his own strong hands. He wanted to smooth away that smudge with his fingers and kiss the softness of her cheek where it had been.

"Why are you looking at me like that?" asked Susannah. "You don't mind that I'm working along with the men, do you?"

"Well," said Paul in a voice so deep and gruff that it didn't even sound like him, so he cleared his throat, "yes and no. I'm the last person to object to anybody wanting to work."

"That's what I thought." Susannah walked around him and opened her car door, but she didn't get in. She reached into the back seat and pulled out a navy peacoat and put it on. She closed the car door and leaned against it. "I like getting my hands dirty, too." She smiled, a smile of self-satisfaction.

"I guess you think you know what you're doing."

The smile disappeared. "Yes, I think I do."

"You'll have to sign a release, then. If you get hurt doing something around here, my insurance won't cover you. You're not one of the crew."

Susannah tossed her head. "So that's what's worrying you! Of course I'll sign your release, if that will make you happy. But honestly, Paul, I'm not going to get hurt. And even if I did, I wouldn't hold you responsible."

"Uh-huh. That's what they all say." He ran his hand through his hair, confused and feeling at a loss. Was it always going to be like this with the two of them, all this prickliness, when what he most wanted was—

"Truce, Paul," said Susannah softly, as if she had been sharing his thoughts. "I was disappointed when I got back to Kinloch and was told that you were out of town. I'd been looking forward to seeing you again, having you show me what you'd done so far on the house and tell me what more has to be done. I still do want that. But something happened the other day that made me all the more eager, and I just couldn't wait. If you think I jumped the gun, coming over and introducing myself to the guys, I apologize. I want the two of us to get along, to work well together."

"Me, too," Paul admitted.

The sun was almost gone. The sky, which in this high place seemed so close overhead, was streaked with long wisps of cloud that were a deep peach color underneath and lavender on top. The air was purple and still—not a sound marred the quiet coming of night. Paul took a step toward Susannah.

"This is a lovely place," she said, gazing around her. "I don't know that I've ever seen any place in the world more beautiful than this."

"Yes," he agreed, and took another step. Susannah's gaze came to rest on his face. Her eyes met his, and held. Her lips parted. Paul's heart beat like thunder in his chest.

Suddenly, out of the gathering darkness, came a black-and-silver streak, tearing toward them. Susannah cringed against her car, eyes wide. A gasp escaped from her parted lips.

It was not what Paul had had in mind for those parted lips. He reached out and held Wolf by her collar. "This is Wolf."

The dog barked and pranced in Paul's grasp.

"Wolf, sit!" Paul commanded, letting her go.

Wolf sat, panting and smiling, her yellow eyes glowing.

"It—it really does look like a wolf!"

"Wolf is a she, not an it. Wolf, this is Susannah. Susannah, come here and give me your hand. I want her to get to know you, to recognize your scent."

But Susannah stayed rooted to her spot. She had laced her hands together so tightly that the knuckles were white. "She doesn't bite, does she?"

"If she doesn't know you, and you make a move that she interprets as threatening to me, she might. She'd growl first—she'd warn you. But if she knows you're my friend, she'll not only accept you, she'll defend you the same as she would me. Come on, give me your hand." Paul moved the few steps between himself and Susannah, saying to Wolf as he did so, "Stay!"

Susannah let Paul take her hand. It was freezing cold. He warmed her hand for a moment in his. Paul looked down at Susannah, but not into her eyes. They were fastened on his dog. "Come on," he urged. It was very important to him that Susannah and Wolf take to each other, though Paul didn't dare analyze why.

Step by tiny step Susannah approached the huge dog. She held Paul's hand so tightly that it almost hurt him. Wolf was alert, her yellow eyes moving from Paul to Susannah, from Susannah to Paul. At last they were close enough. Paul held out his own hand, with Susannah's cupped inside. "This is Susannah," Paul said again. "She's a friend."

With one last keen look at her master, Wolf sniffed Susannah's hand. Susannah trembled—Paul felt the tremor pass down her arm—but she held her ground. Slowly, she let her hand relax, the fingers open up. Wolf pushed her nose into Susannah's palm.

"Oh-h-h," breathed Susannah, "I think she likes me." Wolf was now licking her hand.

"Of course she does, because *I* like you," said Paul. His voice had gone mysteriously gruff again. He let go of Susannah's hand and stepped back.

"She's so big and so gorgeous," marveled Susannah, her fear forgotten. She knelt in order to be closer to Wolf, then rubbed the dog's head, her ears, and stroked her back. "You're such a great, strong, wonderful dog!"

Wolf made a sound of contentment that was almost a purr as she nuzzled Susannah's neck and licked her cheek.

"You do like me, don't you, you gorgeous thing!"

Susannah rubbed, Wolf nuzzled and licked, and Paul's groin burned while his heart pounded. Wolf more than had her scent, now she would never forget this woman. Nor would he.

# Chapter Five

Susannah became obsessed with Laird's Mount. This didn't bother her—obsession was a stage she went through on any project that truly had her interest. She would eat, sleep and breathe it, until at last she was satisfied with the quality of her work. Though she hadn't designed Laird's Mount herself, she felt tremendous admiration for the eighteenth-century gentleman who had. She felt that she was sharing in his pride as she discovered more and more excellence in the construction. The brick walls were as solid as rock. An amazing thirty-inches thick for the outer walls, half that for the inner walls. It made the house impervious to those two scourges of early buildings—termites and fire. And there was the unusual innovation of built-in cabinetry. Where, in 1790-something had he learned that? The tall windows were cleverly placed to reveal the vista that unfolded behind the house and to capture cooling breezes in summer. The high ceilings would hold that coolness, and huge chimneys would warm the house in winter. The fireplaces in every room were set in surrounds of beautiful marble, their mantelpieces magnificently carved. The rooms were so perfectly balanced and proportioned that even in the midst of construction debris Susannah could tell that the house would be a joy to inhabit. The more she saw, the more she rejoiced, as the gentleman himself must have rejoiced.

Paul had taken her to the basement, where he showed her that Laird's Mount was built on a foundation of solid rock. He'd determined that the rock extended to a depth of five feet. He showed her an ancient, clever system of bringing water from a nearby well through a wooden pipe that looked as if it had been hollowed out from a single tree trunk. The well, though covered over now, still provided water by a modern water pump. Paul admired the builder as much as Susannah did. He said that most of the restoration work so far had been removal of inferior nineteenth- and twentieth-century "improvements." Yet Paul balked when Susannah said effusively that the original builder had been a natural-born architect, ahead of his time.

If only Paul weren't so prickly! Susannah hadn't yet told him that she wanted to live in Laird's Mount, and she wasn't sure why—probably because of that touchiness. He was happy enough to show her around, but uncomfortable letting her work alongside him and his crew, in spite of the fact that she'd signed his release. When she'd asked to see his drawings and lists and timetables, Paul had produced them with a kind of pugnacious anxiety, as if he expected her to grade him. He was a superior draftsman, and Susannah had said so, yet her obsessive desire to move into the house as soon as possible made her question Paul's timetables without telling him the reason for it. He hadn't liked that and hadn't given her a direct answer.

Susannah decided to turn her attention to the history of Laird's Mount. She wanted to know everything, especially about that natural-born architect with whom she now identified. Earlier, Paul had said her mother had done a lot of research, so there were bound to be notes. Papers. Susannah asked Paul, but he didn't have them, he'd only heard verbal reports from Jane. So where were Jane's research papers?

As Susannah finished her morning run, she thought about this. Surely her mother would have written down the results of her research, but Susannah hadn't seen anything about Laird's Mount when she'd gone through the contents of her mother's desk. Of course, that had been weeks ago and she'd been looking for only the doctor's name, which she'd found fairly quickly. The deed to Laird's Mount had been in the safety-deposit box at the bank, but no other papers pertaining to the old house had been there.

*I'll just have to look through Mother's desk again,* Susannah thought as she walked the last block back to the Judge's house, cooling down. She did her usual series of end-run stretches out on the lawn, in spite of a cold, blustery wind. Delaying her entry, delaying the necessity of seeing her father, whose general air of depression and hopelessness got to her, and also got her down. Access to Jane's desk might be a problem, Susannah realized as she pushed open the front door.

The desk was in the master bedroom, and the Judge spent more and more time in bed these days.

"SUSANNAH, IS THAT YOU?" The tall, once-stately but now bent form of Judge Harold Hathaway hesitated in the doorway of the room he'd shared with his wife.

"Yes, Judge, it's me," said Susannah from her place on the floor. He was frowning, a strained expression on his face. In God's name, when would he admit that he could barely see? She suppressed an impatient sigh—she'd hoped the Judge would stay longer in his study—and pushed her hair out of her eyes. She was going through the drawers in the lower part of Jane's antique secretary desk. "I'm looking for something in Mother's desk. I've almost finished. If you want to lie down, I'll come back later to finish up."

"That's all right. You go ahead." The Judge shuffled into the room, trailing one hand against the wall, touching furniture—a highboy chest, the corner of the dresser, a bedpost—on his way to a pair of boudoir chairs that flanked a tea table in front of the bedroom's bay window. Susannah tried not to watch him, it was too painful.

The Judge lowered himself into the chair, took a book from under his arm and opened it on the table. Then he gazed in Susannah's direction. "What are you looking for?"

"Paul Starbuck told me that Mother did a lot of research on Laird's Mount before they started the restoration. I'd really like to know what she learned. I thought she must have written it down, or collected some papers, or *something*. But so far, I've found nothing like that." Susannah thought, but did not say, that Jane's desk was cluttered with the kind of personal memorabilia that ought to be donated to charity or thrown out after someone dies. The Judge wouldn't do it, or allow anyone else to do it. Jane's clothes still hung in the double closet, still lay folded in the chest of drawers. Surely that was unhealthy, even morbid. The Judge had been through these drawers himself, Susannah was sure of it. The contents showed signs of having been rifled through.

"Humph," said the Judge. Susannah glanced at him. He turned his head away, toward the window.

Susannah pulled out the bottom drawer, which was in worse disarray than the others had been. The contents looked promising in that they were all papers of one kind and another, but what a mess! Jane, who'd been neat to the point of meticulousness, would not have left any drawer in this condition, that was for certain.

"You know, Judge," said Susannah, unable to keep a hint of peevishness from her voice, "this whole thing would be a lot easier if you would give me a little help!"

"What whole thing?"

Susannah hadn't really expected a response—her father so often ignored anything she said. She opened her mouth to answer, and more than she'd intended to say came out. "*This* whole thing. You. Me. Life after Mother!"

"There is no such thing as life after your mother," said Judge Hathaway wearily. "I'm old, I'm going blind, there's no point to living anymore without my Jane."

Inside her head Susannah was screaming, *But I'm here, I'm alive. I'm your daughter and you don't even know me!* But what she said was, "I understand how you feel."

"I doubt it," said the Judge dismissively, directing his unseeing eyes once more out the window.

Susannah got to her feet, nervously clenching and unclenching her fists. She crossed the room and sat in the other chair, intensely, uncomfortably aware that it was where Jane would have sat. She cleared her throat. She said, "I'm not an idiot, Father." She had never in memory called him Father before.

Startled, the Judge turned his face to Susannah and tried to focus on her.

She pressed on. "Mother often told me that I inherited more from you than my height and my coloring. She said I have your intelligence, and your strength of character." If that was true, why was she so weak in the knees all of a sudden and why were her hands starting to sweat?

"I never doubted your intelligence, Susannah, and I have in the past observed your unfortunate resemblance to me."

At the coldness in his voice Susannah's heart tried to curl up around the edges, to shrivel and die, but she wouldn't let it. Nor would she allow the image of Jane's pretty face to enter her mind. "My point is that I do understand your feelings better than you realize. I know you're going blind, and I also know that it isn't permanent, any more than your depression is. For God's sake, Judge, I'm trying to make a life for myself here in Kinloch, and to make this transition a little smoother for you! That's all, and I really could use some encouragement."

For several heart-thumping minutes, the Judge said not a word. At last he spoke. "I don't intend to encourage you, Susannah. I think you should have stayed in Cambridge. I did not ask you to move in here with me. I was never much of a father to you, and it's too late to start now. I prefer being alone."

"You've certainly made that abundantly clear," said Susannah, matching him tone for tone. "Well, don't worry. I intend to move into Laird's Mount as soon as I can. I'll be around, but I won't be underfoot. I expect that will be better for both of us." She got up from the chair. "Now, if you don't mind, I'll finish going through these drawers."

The Judge's voice, oddly halting, stopped her when she was even with the foot of the bed. "I think... someone... has been there before you."

"What?" She whipped around, astonished.

"I'm not sure. I, ah... I heard something. One afternoon, during that time you'd gone back to Cambridge. I didn't pay much attention at first, I was dozing in the chair in my study. I don't sleep much at night, you know, so sometimes..." The Judge's voice trailed off while Susannah waited for him to continue; she hardly dared to breathe. He roused himself and went on. "I heard it again and then I remembered. That woman, the cook, Sarah, said she was going to the grocery store. I should have been alone in the house. I went out in the hallway and listened. I can't see much, but there's nothing wrong with my ears. I heard rustling sounds, coming from this room. I called out something like 'Tom, are you in there?' but I didn't think it was Tom. I just wanted to put a scare into whoever it was."

"You should have called the police!"

The Judge shrugged. "I suppose so. I didn't care to. I don't care very much about anything these days. I hung back in a doorway and watched, and somebody—I guess it was a man, I can only see shapes now—came out and went down the hall and out the back door. That was the end of it, no intruders since."

Susannah was disbelieving—a former criminal court judge, depressed or not, couldn't observe an intruder and do nothing! "You didn't go through Mother's desk yourself? Certainly somebody did, the drawers aren't as neat as she would have kept them."

"No, I didn't. Nor do I know anything about any research your mother may have done on Laird's Mount. I discouraged Jane's talking about it with me. I never liked the idea of her getting involved with all that restoration business. Took too much of her time. Now it's taking too much of your time. No good will come of it—look what happened to Jane. Finish with the drawers if you must, then let me rest, Susannah."

With shaking hands, Susannah sifted through the haphazard collection of papers in the bottom drawer. Had there really been an intruder here, in this room, and if so, had he gone through Jane's desk drawers? The Judge's story was simply too fantastic to credit. No, more likely he'd fallen asleep in his chair and dreamed the whole thing.

Nevertheless, Susannah did not find a single paper relating to Laird's Mount among her mother's things.

LATER THAT SAME AFTERNOON, Susannah offered to help Sarah prepare dinner. She'd never been very interested in cooking and consequently wasn't much good at it, but there was something about Sarah that attracted her. Susannah sat quietly on a tall stool at the kitchen counter, stringing beans the way Sarah had demonstrated. These moments in the kitchen were filled with a quiet contentment that was pleasantly at odds with the older woman's quick, efficient movements. The contentment had to come from Sarah—it certainly wasn't emanating from Susannah herself— and she was grateful for it.

After a while Susannah broke the peaceful silence, asking, "Sarah, do you know anything about Laird's Mount?"

"I reckon so." Sarah shifted her eyes quickly to Susannah. "Like what kind of thing?"

"Oh, who built it, who has lived there since, any stories or legends about the place."

"Round here, we just call it the Mount. As to who built it, I dunno. I 'spect there's an ol' graveyard up there somewhere—most of them ol' places have graveyards. I 'spect you could find him buried with his name on the stone.''

"I never thought of that! I'll look, first thing tomorrow. But go on, Sarah. Tell me whatever you know.''

"They're lots of stories. Don' know if there's any truth to 'em.'' Sarah looked at her again, keeping her hands moving—she was mixing dough in a bowl for dinner rolls.

"I don't care if it's gospel truth or not, really.''

"Well, they do say as how the man who built the Mount, he done overreached himself. Made himself a grand house an' all, but he used up all his money on it. His life went bad after that.'' Sarah shook her head. "Weren't never no happiness in the Mount, Susannah. Say his wife left him, ran off with another man or some such. Didn't have no children to carry on. Then some other people bought it, an' so on. Times between, that big place stay empty. Seems like nobody stays there for long. Then, back in my grandmama's time—'' Sarah dusted flour from her palms and put her hands on her hips. "I don' know as I should be tellin' you these things, Miss Susannah.''

"Just Susannah, remember, and yes, since the Mount belongs to me now, you most definitely should be telling me. Go on, please.''

"Well, back in my grandmama's time there was a bad man lived there, a mean son of a gun, but he was rich. He had a lot of people workin' for him so ever'-body heard tell what went on. He beat his wife, poor woman, an' she died young. Left him with two boys. Those boys were downright peculiar, didn't neither one of 'em ever marry, they grew up and kep' on living right there in that big house with their mean daddy till he was an ol', ol' man. Then he died and those boys—they were kinda ol' men themselves by then— they stayed on. I think they were twins, but I ain't rightly sure about that. Anyway, those boys let all the help go, they didn't have any sharecroppers or nuthin', they just kept on livin' off their daddy's money.''

Sarah paused, staring at nothing. "Lemme see, can I remember the name? Yes, was Richardson. Story was—now mind, I don' know if it's true or not—how one of those Richardson twins lorded it over the other one. Maybe even kilt him, 'cause one of those twins died, but it was awhile afore anybody knew it. They say that one is the ghost.''

"Ghost?" An involuntary chill ran down Susannah's spine.

"Yes'm. I ain't never seen it, but I know some who have. It's true fact that since the last Richardson died, ain't nobody lived in the Mount. It's been standin' empty for a good thirty years afore your mama bought the place.''

"I'd heard that myself, but I don't think a ghost had anything to do with it. Jane bought the Mount—from the Richardson family. The heirs, the ones who inherited it thirty years ago, just didn't get around to deciding what to do with the property until recently. They live out West, and as you said, that family ap-

pears to have plenty of money. I guess they just forgot about it.''

Sarah shook her head, then turned the dough in its
bowl and covered it with a clean dish towel. ''I reckon
as how it could be better for you, Susannah, if it'd
stayed forgotten. Not to mention better for yo' poor
mama, God rest her soul!''

YOU HAD TO GIVE Dr. Marvin Bradley credit for one
thing: he was persistent. He kept after Susannah to
have dinner with him. She didn't want to encourage
him because she sensed that he wasn't the type of man
who would be interested in building a simple friend-
ship with a woman, so she kept saying no. In a weak
moment, more worried about the Judge than she liked
to admit, and wanting a different perspective from
Sarah's about the Mount, she caved in and said yes.
She even broke her own rule about driving herself the
first time out with a new man, rationalizing that the
doctor wasn't really ''new.'' She did feel as if she knew
him—more or less—and besides, he was a doctor.
Hardly a likely candidate for date rape.

He arrived in a doctor-type car that was only a tad
smaller than her father's Lincoln. ''I've made reser-
vations at the Inverness Inn. If you haven't been there
before, I think you're in for a pleasant surprise. The
food is excellent.''

Susannah merely smiled politely, unwilling to say
that she'd had dinner there with Paul Starbuck. Being
enclosed in a car with Marvin Bradley made her a lit-

tle nervous. She wondered how she would get through the evening.

Across the table from him in the subdued, candlelit atmosphere of the Inn's dining room, Susannah acknowledged that the man had his own brand of charm. Especially when he curved those voluptuous lips in a smile. The food was truly delicious, and the wine loosened her tension as well as her tongue. During the usual getting-to-know-you exchange he said little about himself, but was adept at drawing her out.

Refusing dessert in favor of decaffeinated coffee, Susannah at last felt able to raise the subjects she wanted to talk about. "I need some advice, Marvin."

His pale, protuberant eyes probed Susannah's. "Not medical advice, I hope."

"Oh," she said hastily, "not about me. I have two things on my agenda, actually, and only the first is medical related. I do hope you'll hear me out because I really need help."

Marvin Bradley assumed his listening position, elbows on the table and fingertips pressed together. "I wouldn't think of refusing a damsel in distress. Do proceed."

"First, my father. I think he's depressed, but I can't get him to do anything about it. The frame of mind he's in, I'm afraid he won't even have the cataract surgery when the time comes. He seems resigned to going blind. He's listless, lethargic, but as strong-willed as ever. Right now he's using his strength of will to isolate himself in his grief over Jane's death. I'm sure it's not healthy, but there's not a chance in the world that I could get him to see even you, much less a psychiatrist. What do you suggest?''

"Hmm. It's a trifle unorthodox, but I suppose I could prescribe an antidepressant without examining him. Judge Hathaway is on my patient roster, though I've only seen him twice. As I remember, except for the cataracts, he was in good physical health. Is that still the case?''

"I think so.''

"What about sleeping? Eating?''

"His sleeping pattern is definitely abnormal. He says he doesn't sleep well at night, but I don't know about that. I do know that he sleeps too much in the daytime. As for eating—he'll eat when food is put in front of him, but left on his own, I doubt he'd bother. I've hired a couple, Tom and Sarah Parrish, to help out at home. Sarah is a wonderful cook, and she sees to it that he has balanced, regular meals.''

The doctor pulled his fingertips apart, then put them together again, one, two, three times while he stared off over Susannah's head. He resumed eye contact when he'd apparently reached a conclusion. "What you describe are classic symptoms of situational depression. I'll review the Judge's chart for height and weight to determine the proper dosage, and write a prescription for one of the proven antidepressants. You can come by and pick it up about noon tomorrow.''

"Oh, thank you!'' Susannah experienced a flood of relief.

"But you must promise me something.''

"All right, if I can."

"You must—this is essential. When the Judge has been on the medication for a few days—that is, assuming you can get him to take it—he should feel considerably better. His appetite will improve, and so on. The lethargy will lift. When you observe these changes, you must insist that he come to see me so that I can monitor him. We won't want to continue the antidepressant for any longer than necessary."

Susannah looked dubious. "Depressed or not, the Judge can be awfully stubborn. I don't suppose you make house calls?"

Marvin Bradley drew back, looking down his long, thin nose. "I certainly do not. If I made an exception for your father, I'd soon have to be running out to visit everyone with a cold in this town!"

"I see your point. Okay, I promise. Somehow, I'll get him there."

"Agreed. Now, you said there were two things on your agenda. Before we get to the second, will you have an after-dinner drink?"

Susannah felt that obtaining the doctor's help for her father's depression was cause for a small celebration, so she agreed. "Yes, that would be nice."

Marvin signaled the waiter and ordered the drinks. As soon as the waiter departed she broached her second problem.

"The other thing concerns my house, Laird's Mount. Sarah Parrish told me they call it just the Mount, and she also told me some of the local stories. I'd like to get another perspective, and I thought you might be the one to provide it since you have had a long-standing interest in the place."

"What do you mean, another perspective?" Dr. Bradley's large eyes seemed guarded, wary.

"On the history of the house. Who has lived there since the original builder, that kind of thing. Oh, I did find out who built it. Sarah said there might be a graveyard on the property, and there is. When I get to the landscape part of the restoration, I'll have the old graveyard cleaned up and refenced. The builder's name was Cunningham. I expect you knew that."

The drinks had come while Susannah spoke. Marvin Bradley lifted the small, slender glass and drained half of it in one inelegant swig. Strange, thought Susannah, not at all in keeping with the fastidious manners he'd displayed during the meal. She noticed how the thick liquid of the crème de menthe he'd ordered still clung to his lush lips, giving them a greenish shine that was slightly sickening. His tongue, long and sensual, came out to slowly lick those lips. Susannah lowered her eyes as she sipped her own considerably less sweet liqueur.

"Cunningham," said Bradley. "The name means nothing to me. I, ah, I don't know much about that house."

"But you said, that day I came to your office back in December, that you were interested in it. In fact, you said you'd been trying to buy it for years."

The doctor downed the remainder of his drink and repeated the business with lips and tongue. Susannah was beginning to feel a strange sort of fascination with the man.

"In my case, the definition of years is not so long as you apparently think, Susannah. I have been here less than five years. I got into medicine rather later than most of my colleagues, and my interest in Laird's Mount is not of the historical variety. It's simply that it's the finest house in town, and I have an appreciation of fine things." As he said this his eyes roamed over her body, including her in the category of fine things.

She felt as if he were touching her all over, a disturbing feeling that she tried to ignore. "I admit I'm disappointed. You see, my mother did some research on the history of the Mount, but either she didn't write down her findings or what she did write has been lost."

"What does it matter? And as long as we're on this subject, how can I persuade you to sell?"

"I suppose you must be the client that Realtor, Charles Herbert, has waiting in the wings."

"Could be." Marvin Bradley leaned over the table. "But we could leave him out, save us both some money. You could sell directly to me. You can trust me to complete the restoration in the best possible manner. Really, Susannah, I must have that house!"

"I—I'm afraid you can't." Susannah felt like she was under a spell. The man was mesmerizing, but he also nauseated her. "I'm going to move in as soon as things are far enough along for me to live there." Susannah remembered Sarah's stories, and that gave her pause. "At least, that's what I've been planning. Are you sure you haven't heard anything at all, you know, around town? I mean, about the ghost, for instance?"

"Ah! The ghost!" The doctor leaned even closer. His eyes glittered. "All these old houses are reputed to have a ghost or two. I'm convinced there is one at Laird's Mount, and it's malevolent. In fact—" he lowered his voice to an intimate, conspiratorial pitch "—I fully believe that the ghost of Laird's Mount killed Jane Hathaway. Your mother."

# Chapter Six

Paul Starbuck carefully placed another log on the fire and stood back, rubbing his hands together in satisfaction. He and Susannah were in the larger of the two first-floor rooms in the main block of Laird's Mount. Except for some minor plaster repair, painting and floor refinishing, the work in this room was complete. The chimneys had been inspected and cleaned early on, but still, you could never be sure a chimney would draw until you tried it. Having a fire in here at the end of the workday had been Susannah's suggestion.

"So," he said beaming, pleased with the fire and himself, "what do you think?"

"I think," said Susannah, holding out her hands to the flames, "that in this climate, with such huge fireplaces, I won't really need a furnace! This is wonderful, Paul. Thank you."

Paul looked down at Susannah. She sat on the floor in front of the fire, legs folded, on a plaid blanket he kept in his truck. She was wearing jeans and a dark green wool shirt. Her socks were dark green, too—

she'd removed an old pair of running shoes and put them off to the side. Her honey-colored hair was tousled from work she'd done earlier. She'd been sweeping out this room and the one next to it. He wanted to get close to her. "Mind if I join you down there?"

"Of course not." She smiled up at him. Paul sat down next to her, carefully leaving a foot or so between them. Susannah looked at him, a serious expression in her gray eyes. "It's time we talked about a few things."

"I'm game."

"I've been making some plans, and I need to know a couple of things from you. Such as, what's the status of the bathrooms in this house?"

Paul rubbed the back of his head, feeling instantly mulish. "I showed you the plans, remember? We'll have two new bathrooms on the second floor—one for each bedroom in the gabled space over the side wings. That gets done last, after the restoration work is finished. I won't do it myself, but I'll get you a good subcontractor. You'll have a ball picking out fixtures and stuff. The bathrooms will be huge—"

"That's not what I meant. Those will be new. I'm asking about the old bathrooms. Where were they, and can at least one of them be made usable temporarily?"

"Oh." Paul rubbed his head some more. "You remember I told you how much time we spent tearing out inferior additions?" Susannah nodded. "Well, the bathrooms were added in about the 1920s, and they were really terrible. I tore them out. They're long gone.''

"Well, could you put one back? Down here? I really do think I'll want a small bathroom on the first floor, anyway.''

Paul studied Susannah's face. She was up to something. This wasn't just about bathrooms. "What exactly is on your mind, Susannah?"

She pulled her knees up and wrapped her arms around them. Paul admired the long line of her thighs, and the way her hair swung forward when, for a moment, she rested her forehead against her knees. She sighed. "I've been dreading telling you this. I'm afraid you'll think I'm rushing you, and I don't mean to. Really, I don't.''

"So tell me. Whatever it is, I can handle it.''

"I'd like to move in here, in these two rooms. I won't mind the rest of the restoration work going on around me. I can do with a makeshift kitchen, but I have to have a proper bathroom. I can't very well go outside to the portable toilet, and I need a place to shower and wash my face.''

"Susannah, are you nuts? You have a large, almost new house to live in with your father. Why in the world would you want to move in here before we get finished? It'll be noisy, dusty, cold and inconvenient.''

"Not cold. I have the fireplace,'' Susannah said calmly.

"Oh, jeez!'' For a minute Paul wanted to whack some sense into her. But then he saw that the shimmer in Susannah's eyes was not a glare but the beginning of tears. She held her chin high, but it quivered faintly. His heart melted, his voice became soft. "Okay, so you have a good reason. Want to tell me what it is?"

One tear—only one—slid down Susannah's cheek. She blinked the rest back, swallowed hard, took a deep breath and said, "I need to get away from my father. He doesn't want me there, he said so. He wants to be alone."

Paul thought of his own big, bearish, affectionate dad, and couldn't imagine what Susannah must be going through. He moved a little closer. "That must be rough."

"Yeah. On me, and him, too." Susannah hung her head. Her hair, glowing with firelight, swung forward and hid her face while she continued to speak. "He's depressed, but I think he'll be okay now. I got him some medication. And he has Sarah and Tom Parrish to look after him. I won't leave him entirely alone, I'll check in with him every day. But I have to get out of there, I can't breathe in that house!"

"Okay, okay," Paul soothed, instinctively moving to comfort Susannah in the way he would have comforted one of his own sisters. He put his arm around her and drew her in so that she leaned against him. He took it for granted that she wouldn't resist. He stroked her hair, murmuring low. "We'll work something out. You don't have to stay there anymore, we'll make a place for you. Everything will be fine."

But everything was not fine. In response to Paul's kindness, Susannah began to cry. At first she whimpered, like a wounded animal. Paul was baffled. Then, in a flash, his earlier insight came back to him of the uncertain, unhappy little girl locked up inside the tall, proud body of Susannah Hathaway. He whispered, "Go ahead, let it out. I understand."

"I'm sorry," she gulped. The gulp turned into a ragged sob. She said, between sobs, "I don't know what's wrong with me!" She tried to struggle out of Paul's arm, but he held her fast.

"I think maybe I do," said Paul. He sensed that all Susannah's life she'd done that, fought down tears, battled bad feelings without help. With infinite tenderness, he drew her closer still, pressing her head against his big shouder. He said, "Cry, Susannah. Let go... let go... let go."

NIGHT FELL AS PAUL HELD Susannah in his arms. Black shadows appeared in the room at Laird's Mount, around their charmed circle of fire and warmth. He rocked gently, slowly, back and forth, cradling her as on and on she cried.

Susannah could not remember the last time she'd felt so helpless. No matter how hard she tried, she could not stop crying. She kept hearing that deep, soothing voice encouraging her to let go... let go. At last something inside her broke, let go completely, and she gave herself up to the tears.

He was rocking her. Nobody ever rocked her! She had her fingers twisted in the fabric of his shirt. Underneath her cheek, his shirt was wet with her tears. He didn't complain. His arms were strong. He still rocked, and he hummed. That humming tugged the corners of Susannah's mouth upward—Paul couldn't carry a tune in a bucket, but there was no doubt he hummed a lullaby. Susannah closed her eyes. The tears had stopped, but surely there was no harm in letting him hold her like this, just a little longer.

"YOU CRIED A BIT, then you fell asleep," said Paul.

"How long?" Susannah disentangled herself from his arms. Remembering, she put her hand on his shirt where her head had been—it was still damp. Still half-asleep, she looked at Paul in wonder.

"Not long. Maybe half an hour."

It had gotten dark. She should be embarrassed, she'd acted like such a fool. But she wasn't embarrassed, she felt wonderful. Clean inside. And safe, here in the circle of the fire's light. She remembered how safe she had felt in Paul's arms. His deep blue eyes, catching the light, shone like star sapphires. "Thank you," she said.

"No problem. Feeling better now?"

"Yes, but—"

"Like I said, no problem. Don't apologize. I understand. You needed to cry. No big deal."

No big deal, he said, and yet to her it was. It was a very big deal to have been held and comforted, rocked to sleep, sung a lullaby. Such simple kindness she had never known, from anyone. She had to tell him, somehow. "No one has ever done anything like that for me before. I—I don't know what to say."

"You already said it, and you're welcome. Now, the question is, what are we going to do to help you out of your, er, situation? I was thinking about it while you were sleeping, and this is what I came up with. There's a big walk-in pantry in the next room—"

"The one we're going to make into a kitchen and breakfast room?"

"Right. And I can take about two-thirds of that pantry space for a small bathroom. I'm sure we can get one of those Fiberglas shower-stall units in there. Five days, Susannah. If I'm lucky and can get the plumbing contractor I use to come over right away, we might do it in three. There's another alternative, though."

"What?"

"We'll be through with the whole restoration, except for that mess on the third floor, in two to three months. You'd be a heck of a lot more comfortable if you just moved into the Inverness Inn until then." Paul gestured at the reach of darkness in the high-ceilinged room, at the night pressing up against the uncurtained windows. "You might not like being out here all by yourself without a telephone and an alarm system. It's isolated, and it's also pretty damn spooky."

"The electricity will be hooked up any time now, and then it won't seem so dark. I can get a telephone."

"Not as easy as you think. The Mount has never had phone service. The phone company will have to run a line all the way out here, and that'll take God knows how much time."

"We won't know until we try, will we? Anyway, I don't want to go to the Inn. I already thought of that alternative and rejected it. Really, Paul, if you could go ahead with that bathroom in the three to five days you mentioned, I'd be very grateful. I'll be fine here, I know I will."

"You left one thing out."

"What, you mean the alarm system? I hardly think I need one in Kinloch."

"I meant about it being spooky. It is, you know."

She tossed her head. An unwelcome little knot formed in her stomach. "I don't get spooked easily."

"Yeah, I was afraid you'd say that. Look, Susannah, let's talk about that a little more, but not here." Paul looked over his shoulder, into the darkness. He stood up and reached a hand out to her. "Tell you what, come back with me to my place. Wolf is going to be wondering where I am. I'll cook you some dinner. I'm a pretty good cook."

When Paul grinned like that he was very nearly irresistible. Susannah let him pull her to her feet. For just a moment, she wished she were back in his arms again. His eyes softened, he kept her hand. Maybe he wished it, too. Her voice cracked a little as she said, "We could go out. You don't have to cook for me."

"I want to," Paul said gruffly, dropping her hand. He bent down and swept up the blanket. "Here, don't forget your shoes."

SUSANNAH COULDN'T HELP but contrast this dinner with the one she'd had with another man—Dr. Marvin Bradley—two nights earlier. The differences boggled her mind. For one thing, there was Wolf. She wondered idly how Wolf would take to the strangely sensual Dr. Bradley, and decided the dog wouldn't take to him at all. Or vice versa. And she was pretty sure that Dr. Bradley would look down his long, thin nose at Paul's little house with its pine-paneled walls, multicolored braided rug and motley collection of comfortable furniture. For that matter, so would her father. He preferred a certain degree of elegance, Oriental rugs, antique furniture—

"Oh!" Susannah exclaimed, "where's your telephone? I have to call and make sure the Judge is all right. I should have been there a couple of hours ago."

"It's in here," Paul called from the kitchen alcove.

Susannah made her call. She should not have been surprised to hear the Judge say, "Whatever you do is your own concern, Susannah." He hadn't missed her at all. She guessed she should be glad he'd bothered to answer the phone.

"Hey—" Paul nudged her with his elbow, his hands occupied with chopping up something "—did you find the candles?"

"Yes." She tossed her hair out of her eyes and forced the Judge out of her thoughts. "You have quite an assortment. I'm still choosing. When I'm done with that, I'll set the table.''

"Great. This will be done in a few minutes.''

Paul's candles were not the tall tapers that require candelabra. They came in a variety of shapes and heights and colors, from fat pillar candles to free-form sand castings to tiny votives in lovely colored glasses. All had been burned many times; in fact, some of them probably should have been thrown out, but she could see why he'd kept them. They were lovely. As Susannah made her choices, she thought about Paul Starbuck, the single man. Surely a man did not go out and buy candles like these for himself. How many women had been in his life? Had he ever been married? Did he really like her as much as she was beginning to hope he might, or was he just being kind?

Wolf pawed at the door, and Susannah got up to let the dog in as casually as if she'd been doing it every day of her life. "Woof!" said the gorgeous creature, prancing in.

"The same to you, I'm sure," Susannah replied. She impulsively went down on her knees and hugged Wolf, burying her face in the dog's thick, shaggy coat. Invigorated by her run in the brisk night air, Wolf wanted to play. She taught Susannah how, nudging and pawing and romping.

"Five minutes!" Paul warned from the kitchen.

Susannah, laughing, pushed Wolf away. "Enough! I've got to set the table now." The dog followed her new playmate into the bathroom where she washed her hands, then into the kitchen where she found silverware and plates, and back into the dining area at one side of the living room. Wolf cocked her head to one side and observed with interest as Susannah lighted the candles she'd chosen and placed in the center of the table.

"Ready or not, here it comes," Paul announced.

In half an hour he had thrown together a stir-fry that was delicious. Susannah ate ravenously.

"My mom always said that after a good cry you need a big meal," Paul observed. "Obviously, she was right."

Susannah grew somber. "I don't think I've ever cried like that before."

Paul's eyes met hers. "Then it was time."

"Yes. You're right, it was time." Susannah sighed, putting down her fork. "And I couldn't possibly eat another bite. It was delicious, Paul. Thank you. Thank you for everything you've done tonight." She wondered how she'd ever thought he was prickly.

He winked, making the moment light. "Just doing what comes naturally."

"You have something special, Paul. I feel it sometimes when I'm with you, and especially here, in the home you've made for yourself. There's so much warmth, unpretentiousness, a self-confidence that you show by the things you've gathered together here. You learned all this, somehow, and I—I never did. Maybe I can learn from you."

Wolf, as if she could read emotions in the air, got up from her place under the table and pushed her head into Susannah's lap, whining softly. Susannah would not have thought she could have a tear left in her body, but she felt her eyes fill again. She looked down, buried a hand in the dog's ruff, and blinked the dampness away.

Paul cleared his throat, then said, "Anything I have to give you, Susannah, I will. Gladly. As it was given to me by my mother and father, brothers and sisters. You've had a hard life, I can see that. It only looks privileged on the surface. If you want to talk about it, I'll listen."

She tried to smile, and didn't quite manage it. "There's not much to say. I figured it out a few years ago, with the help of an expensive but good therapist. The whole problem was that the Judge and my mother had what's called in therapist lingo a symbiotic relationship."

"I've heard of that. A symbiosis is a closed system, where one part feeds the other in a continuous loop."

"Exactly. They appeared to have the perfect marriage, but actually a symbiosis isn't healthy for people. And there's no room in it for a child. The couple loves each other passionately, possessively and exclusively. There's no love left for the child. The Judge and my mother had none for me. I grew up thinking it was somehow my fault that they didn't love me. I know now that it wasn't my fault, that all the good grades in the world, or all the trying to be as beautiful as my mother was—which was impossible, of course—"

"Susannah, look at me. Jane was a beautiful woman, even at her age, and she was attractive to men. But she was not as beautiful as you are. Your beauty is different, it comes from the inside out.''

She heard Paul's words, but couldn't let herself feel their importance. She shook her head out of a long habit of self-denial. She went on, her voice barely above a whisper. It was hard, but it felt so good, so good, to be able to tell this to a person other than a therapist. ''I knew that in my head, but someplace inside I just couldn't give up hoping that somehow, someday I'd be able to make them love me. Especially Mother—she was always more approachable than the Judge. I hoped that when I came here at Christmas... Well, now it's too late. She's gone, and the Judge will never change. I'm so stupid, Paul! I did it again, I got into thinking that with Jane gone, the Judge would need me, that he'd see that he has a daughter who wants to love him—''

''Who wants him to love her.''

''Yes!'' Susannah declared fiercely, her voice suddenly so loud that it seemed to fill the room. Then it sank again to a near-whisper. ''But he never will.''

Paul came around the table. He urged Susannah up and into his arms. He kissed her temple, her cheek, her eyes and, at last, her mouth. His lips were soft, his kiss as gentle as any father's kiss. He was instinctively giving her exactly what she needed. He held the back of her head, pressing her chin into his shoulder, and said compellingly in her ear, ''You're a woman now, Susannah. You don't need your father's love anymore. Believe me, you don't.''

Susannah said, ''I believe you.''

Then he kissed her again, this time with a growing, burning ardor that sought and found her equal response. They moved, amid more kisses, from the table to the couch, touching tongues, touching hands, touching skin. When Paul's hand brushed her breast, Susannah's nipples hardened—so suddenly sensitive it was almost painful. She moaned deep in her throat and captured his hand. "No," she said, "no more. Not now. Not tonight."

She could not tell him that if she had not left at that moment, she would never have had the strength to drive herself home.

PAUL SHUT THE BEDROOM door and stared at the ceiling. He hadn't meant to take advantage of Susannah. Probably she'd never allowed herself to be any more vulnerable than she had been with him, tonight. He was glad—well, almost glad—she'd stopped him.

He pounded his fist against his forehead. Damn, he'd come close to telling Susannah that he loved her!

Wolf whined softly at the door. Paul got up and opened it, then lay down again on the bed. After sniffing a few times to make sure nothing was amiss, Wolf padded back out to the braided rug where her rawhide bone waited to be chewed. Paul lay there, trying to figure out if he was really in love with Susannah Hathaway.

One thing was for sure: Susannah brought out both the best and the worst in him. Worst was when he envied all she had in life that she didn't appreciate or take advantage of. Like her architecture degree. The thing that at one time he'd wanted more than anything himself.

The best in him. Yeah, he did have some good points, all of them precisely what Susannah needed . . . though he hadn't realized it until tonight. He was a loving person, he liked to have a chance to be gentle, he liked how it felt going all warm and soft and fuzzy inside, the way he'd felt holding Susannah when she cried, rocking her. He didn't much like sharp, savvy women who went for sex for instant gratification—with protection, of course—and with no strings attached. He got attracted, he got involved, and then he got uninvolved. The reason he'd never married was that he'd never yet been in love with a woman who wanted all the love he had to give. How did he know that? Well, he just did. He always figured one of these days a woman would come along that he could be himself with. And Susannah was that woman.

So okay. He'd made the big leap, the big admission. He wasn't socially in her league, but she didn't seem to care about that. She had advantages he'd never had, but as she'd said herself tonight, he'd had some things he'd always taken for granted, but they were, apparently, advantages Susannah hadn't had. A different kind, but still important. Maybe the most important of all. Paul had been loved, so he knew how to love. Susannah needed love more than anything else. He would love her. And maybe someday, she would love him in return.

God, wouldn't that be something!

The thought excited him, filled him with joy. He leapt off the bed and loped into the living room, shouting, "Hey, Wolf! I'm in love! I'm in love with Susannah!"

It was only much later, when Paul turned out the light on his bedside table and settled down to sleep, that he realized he had forgotten something. Something that might be important. Susannah was planning to move into Laird's Mount in only a few days, and he'd forgotten to tell her about the ghost.

# *Chapter Seven*

Susannah told her father that she would be moving into Laird's Mount within a week's time. She hadn't been entirely sure how he would handle this information; as it turned out, his reaction was disturbing.

Slowly the Judge turned his still-noble head. He stared at Susannah with clouded gray eyes. The book on his lap slid to the floor with a thump as he grasped the arms of his wing chair with both hands, as if he were hanging on for dear life. He said, "That house will kill you, too, Susannah."

"Judge!"

He let out a great sigh, like air from a bellows, then released his grip and slumped back in the chair. "Shouldn't have said that. Don't know what got into me. You do as you please. You're better on your own, anyway."

Susannah had tensed all over; now she began to relax, but not much. Hesitantly she asked, "You don't really think Laird's Mount, the house itself, had anything to do with Mother's death, do you?"

For a long time he didn't answer. Just when Susannah thought he'd slipped back into his own murky world again, he mumbled, "Natural causes. Cardiac arrest." He moved his head back and forth in a gesture of denial and mumbled another phrase. "Never had a superstitious bone in my body."

Susannah's heartbeat quickened. In her obsessive focus on the restoration as a work project, she had suspended earlier concerns about the manner of her mother's death. Now she recalled her first visit to the old house, the feeling that an unseen force was pulling her from room to room and up the stairs; that brief rectangle of light on the floor in the second-floor hall; the certainty, even before Paul had confirmed it, that *that* was the very place Jane had fallen in death. She moistened her lips with the tip of her tongue and asked, "Judge, is there anything—anything at all— that has troubled you about Jane's death and you haven't told me?"

The Judge sighed again. "She changed. From the moment she bought that place, she was different. Not my Jane anymore. I thought—I don't know what I thought. It's just an old house, but I blamed it. Blamed Laird's Mount. I felt it was taking my Jane away from me. Then she died there. There in that cursed house, it took her for good! Leave me alone, Susannah. I'm an old man, I'm not what I used to be. Go wherever you like. Do whatever you want. Leave me in peace."

Susannah swallowed a lump in her throat. She wanted to go to him and kiss his cheek. But the Judge had closed his eyes. She did as he'd asked—she left him there in whatever peace he could find.

As she walked quietly from the study Susannah made a silent promise, to herself and to Jane, wherever she might be. She would not forget. She would find out the truth about her mother's death.

WORD QUICKLY GOT AROUND the small town of Kinloch that Susannah Hathaway was about to move into Laird's Mount, even before the restoration was complete. She probably couldn't have kept her move a secret even if she'd wanted to. The purchase of a few pieces of furniture would have taken care of that. Not to mention pots and pans, a hot plate, dishes...the list grew longer each day. Briefly Susannah wished she'd sublet her apartment unfurnished, but then she realized these few things were nothing, comparatively speaking. She would have a whole house to furnish in the not-too-distant future. And for the first time in her life she wouldn't have to worry about money in the process. Somehow having so much money made her uncomfortable—she was so used to living from paycheck to paycheck.

On a lunch date, Angelica Herbert provided Susannah with suggestions of places to shop. And more than likely, Angelica then provided downtown Kinloch with the news of her impending move. The interested and the curious put themselves in Susannah's path, interrupting her morning runs. Charles Herbert made himself a positive pest. Marvin Bradley gamely tried jogging along with her. Susannah only grinned and waved and wouldn't stop for him. She still didn't know quite what to think of the doctor. He was so peculiar, but not exactly unpleasant.

Paul called and said the electricity had been turned on at last, and the new bathroom was coming along. She should meet with him to approve the fixtures he'd chosen. When they'd met, he'd been touchingly shy, though his dark blue eyes had sparkled. She'd tried to put her emotional behavior the other night out of her mind, but seeing him again brought it all back. Brought back, too, a rush of physical arousal that she repressed by assuming her most professional manner. She thought she'd acted disgracefully with him, quite unlike herself, and intended never to let anything like that happen again.

The day before she was scheduled to move into the Mount, as she completed the loop of the downtown on her morning run and had begun the return trip up St. Andrews Road, Susannah saw a woman standing right in her way.

Susannah nodded by way of greeting and circled out into the road to avoid the woman. No such luck. She thrust out an arm, which Susannah all but ran into. Simultaneously the woman said, "Ms. Hathaway, I think it's time we talked."

*Now?* Susannah was winded from running uphill. She stopped so abruptly that she almost lost her balance. Who was this woman, anyway? "I, ah, have we met?"

"I'm Barbara Blair. I own the big house up the hill there—" she jerked her head "—the bed and breakfast. Of course, it wasn't always that. The house has been in my family for six generations, but I had to go commercial in order to keep it up. More's the pity." She looked Susannah up and down. "Well, don't let's stand here in the road. Come on up and I'll give you juice and coffee, and if you like, a muffin or two. Come on!"

"Well, I guess I can do that," said Susannah doubtfully. Barbara Blair was obviously accustomed to being obeyed. She had turned her back and already crossed the green verge. Susannah stretched her calf and then her thigh muscles before following. She hoped she wouldn't get kinks from stopping her run without a cool down.

Barbara looked back over her shoulder as she began to climb a long, rather steep expanse of lawn. "Are you coming?"

"Yes. Go ahead, I'll catch up." What in the world is this all about? Barbara Blair was probably the same age Jane had been, though in her case she looked it. She was a large woman, stocky rather than fat, and not very tall. When Susannah caught up to her she noted that her hair had probably been red in her youth; now it was faded to a not very attractive gray with a brassy undertone. She had heavy eyebrows of the same faded-brass color, a square jaw with a bit of jowl, and her face wore a stern expression that, judging from its lines and creases, was probably habitual. She puffed with exertion as they climbed her hilly lawn.

"So this is your house," Susannah said when they reached the top. "I'd wondered who lived up here. From the road you can barely see the house for all the trees around it. It's lovely! I didn't know this was a bed and breakfast—there's no sign."

"No need to advertise out front, thank goodness. Having to take in paying guests is humiliating enough in itself. I put ads in the magazines, have a brochure down at the Chamber and all. People find me. So you like my house, do you?"

"Yes, I do," Susannah confirmed. The house was a cross between a Greek Revival mansion and a large farmhouse, with the typical pillared and pedimented portico marking the front entrance. On either side ran a long, deep porch with rows of rocking chairs painted white to match the facade.

"I can take a maximum of ten guests in five bedrooms. Sixth bedroom is mine. There's only four guests here now and they've already eaten. We'll go back to the kitchen." Her last words were accompanied by a quick once-over and a frown of disdain.

Susannah felt her cheeks go pink at what sounded like a criticism. True, her navy blue sweat suit was old and faded, but she hadn't set out expecting to pay social calls! She pulled off her headband, shook her hair out and fluffed it with her fingers, and shoved the headband into her pocket. On her way down the hall she sneaked a look at herself in a tall pier glass. She thought she looked pretty presentable, considering.

"Who did the conversion for you?" asked Susannah, ogling the large modern kitchen with its big restaurant-type appliances. She craned her neck to peer into the dining room, where she saw a magnificent mahogany banquet table with twelve matching chairs, a glass-enclosed breakfront and a buffet.

"Your friend Mr. Starbuck. Here, have a glass of juice and sit down at the table." The table Barbara Blair indicated was round and fit perfectly into the curve of a bow window. Susannah said, "Thank you," and complied with the instructions. She sipped orange juice and looked through the window.

"Is that an old dependency?" she asked, referring to a small rectangular brick building with two tiny windows.

"That's the old kitchen. Because of the heat from cooking and the danger of fire, they didn't put kitchens into houses until plumbing and electricity and all that came in. I use it for a toolshed now."

"Hmm. I have a small building like that at Laird's Mount. I expect it was a kitchen, too, and I've meant to take a look at it, but we've been so busy with the main house I haven't gotten around to it."

A microwave beeped. "Corn muffins. You hungry?"

Susannah nodded. "This is very kind of you. I usually shower and clean up after my run before eating, but—"

"No need to apologize, young lady. I know I've snatched you up, but it seemed the best way. I see you running down there every morning, rain or shine. Seems a peculiar habit to me, but—" she shrugged

"—if you ask me, all young people are peculiar nowadays."

"I don't think of myself as a young person, Mrs. Blair. I'm thirty years old." Nor peculiar, she added to herself.

"To me, that's young. But you can call me Barbara." She sat, smoothed her print housedress over her broad but not very ample bosom, and got down to business. "I don't know as anybody told you, but I'm a founding member of the Kinloch Historical Preservation Society. Your late mother was quite active in our organization. Up to a point."

Mouth full of delicious corn muffin, Susannah raised her eyebrows inquiringly.

"Up to the point when she bought the Mount. Then it suddenly seemed she was too good for us. Now, we welcome you Yankees down here—"

At the word *Yankees* Susannah bristled, but she held her tongue. Kept on chewing, but the muffin was not quite as delicious now.

"—But you might as well know, since we're all aware that you inherited the place from your mother, not to mention that now I hear you're about to move into the Mount yourself, that the society's feelings on the subject of restoring the Mount are divided. About half of us were glad the Richardsons had ignored the place for so long."

Susannah swallowed. "And the other half?"

"I'm in the other half, and we want covenants. Your mother refused to do that. If I do say so myself, she got right uppity there at the end."

As an architect, Susannah was familiar with the concept of restrictive agreements of various kinds. "I have no problem with the idea of historic preservation covenants, Mrs. Blair. Barbara. If you'll have the society's lawyer send me your standard form in the mail, I'll look it over and then we can discuss it."

The stern lines of Barbara's face softened somewhat. "We appreciate that. Now, about you moving into the place. Is that right, you're planning to do it soon, even before Starbuck finishes restoring the house?"

"Yes. Tomorrow, in fact."

"Then I think you should be warned. Since Jane got so uppity, nobody told her, but the word around town is you're a different type, and if you're going to live there, well . . ."

Barbara Blair proceeded to tell Susannah a story not too much different from the one she'd already heard from Sarah Parrish. Susannah heard her through to the end without comment or question. All the while her mind was working a mile a minute. This woman, in spite of her tactlessness, was a gold mine of information.

Accepting a second cup of coffee, Susannah decided to risk a little self-disclosure, in return for which she hoped to learn a lot. "Barbara, I do appreciate everything you've told me. There's no reason you would know this, but I'm an architect by profession. I can't subscribe to the notion that a house, or any type of building, becomes a bad or an unhappy place just because the people who have lived in it have had unfortunate experiences there. I do grant you that sometimes when I've visited old houses—'' Susannah grew thoughtful ''—and especially old churches, in New England, I've felt some kind of energy in them. Almost a presence.''

"That's it. That's the kind of thing I'm talking about," said Barbara on a note of excitement.

"You seem to be suggesting that because the Mount has had people like the Richardson twins living there, the house has become an unpleasant place. Would you go so far as to say malevolent?"

"Oh, no! No, no! Nothing so bad as that, dear me, no. But some people would."

"Ah." Susannah was now nervous, and her mouth had gone dry. She bit her lower lip briefly before proceeding. "Would these same people, by any chance, have a theory about my mother's death at the Mount?"

Barbara Blair's face looked very stern, indeed. She pursed her mouth and said nothing.

Susannah persisted. "Dr. Marvin Bradley, for instance, told me a few nights ago that he believes that my mother, Jane, was frightened to death there. He thinks she saw a ghost, and the experience put such a strain on her heart that she had a cardiac arrest, which was the official cause of her death. I think Charles Herbert was also trying to tell me something similar a few weeks ago, but at the time I thought he just wanted to scare me off from living at the Mount so that I would sell and he could get a fat commission. Now I'm not so sure. What do you think, Barbara?"

Barbara fidgeted with the buttons on the front of her dress. "Since you're asking so directly, I'll tell you. I like a woman who doesn't pussyfoot around. Never could abide a pussyfooter, and we've got way too many of them here in this town. What I think is that if I was you, and I thought maybe my mama didn't exactly die such a natural death as the coroner said, I'd look at a whole lot of other alternatives before I went blaming it on any ghost. Not that there isn't a ghost up there at the Mount, most likely there is, but so what? I've got one, too, right here in this house, she doesn't bother a living soul. Poor thing, I haven't seen her in years, and I hope she's gone on to her eternal rest, but that's another story. I think you'd best go somewhere other than that doctor for your information, too."

"Why is that? I always thought you could trust doctors."

"Humph!" Barbara Blair was now positively enjoying the conversation. "Maybe when I was a girl you could, but not anymore. If it wasn't so hard to get a doctor, any doctor, in a little town like Kinloch . . . Well, he's good enough at his medicine, or seems to be, but you mark my words, young lady, there's more to that Marvin Bradley than meets the eye. If you take my meaning."

Susannah thought so, too, though she hadn't yet been able to put her finger on it. She nodded encouragingly.

"Now, I'm not one to speak ill of the dead—" Barbara stopped, looking uncomfortable.

Taking a breath, hoping she wasn't making a mistake, Susannah said, "I may as well tell you—in confidence—that my mother and I were not close, though I regretted that. I need to know whatever information you have."

"Very well, then. Jane had a way with her. Round about the time folks started thinking she was uppity, your daddy commenced to stay at home a lot. Including on social occasions."

"That's because he isn't exactly well. He's losing his eyesight. But I didn't mean to interrupt you."

"Like I said, Jane had a way with her, and the men in particular responded. If you take my meaning. And Dr. Marvin Bradley, he was among the biggest responders. Charles Herbert was going through a divorce and he responded right smart, too. As for young Starbuck, well, Jane had that boy wrapped around her little finger!"

Susannah felt as if she'd been hit in the stomach.

"I expect your daddy must have known what she was up to. He must be a smart man, being a Judge and all. And mind, I'm not saying Jane was doing anything really, well, immoral. But wrong? Yes, she did wrong to carry on the way she did. And you see, honey, when she started acting like that right about the time she bought the Mount, and began to spend so much time there, what with the Mount having the reputation it has... People put two and two together. Her death didn't come as that much of a surprise to some people, under the circumstances."

Susannah, with a trace of bitterness, put into words what Barbara Blair was undoubtedly thinking. "And some people said that Jane got what she deserved."

*So I learned some things I wish I hadn't learned,* Susannah thought a few minutes later as she walked, not ran, the rest of the way home. She used the long walk to put all the things she'd learned in order. The Judge himself said Jane had changed, and he too connected it with her acquisition of Laird's Mount. How difficult that must have been for him, after all those years of symbiosis! So Jane, in her late fifties, had become a flirt. Surely that's all it was. And even Paul...! Oh, surely not Paul. It mattered to Susannah. She didn't want it to, but it did. She wouldn't think about that.

So Jane had started some kind of relationship with several men, including the very ones who had shown Susannah herself some attention. These were the same men who also seemed to have an interest in the Mount. A rather convoluted picture, hard to decipher. One thing was clear to Susannah—no matter what Jane had done, even if she'd committed adultery several times over, and Susannah doubted that—Jane had not deserved to die. No matter what "some people" said.

As Susannah turned onto the walk up to her father's house, the mental picture she'd been reaching for suddenly became clearer. Petite, pretty Jane Hathaway had stirred up the little town of Kinloch. And the ruling elders, in the sacred enclave of the Historical Preservation Society, had not wanted to be stirred. She had also disrupted her own rock-solid marriage, so you had to count the Judge in with those who were unhappy at being stirred up. Feelings must have run high. How high? High enough that someone had wanted Jane Hathaway out of this picture?

Maybe, Susannah admitted, her hand on the front doorknob. Who? There were several possibilities. How? That was the stumper. How can you kill and not leave a trace?

At least the supposed ghost at Laird's Mount could be discounted, no matter what Marvin Bradley said. The ghost had to be a red herring.

THE NEXT DAY Susannah's few pieces of new furniture were delivered to Laird's Mount, and with Paul's help she brought in the small items she'd bought, plus her clothes. Soon after, she chased Paul off, and Wolf, who had come along to inspect the premises. She wanted to be alone on her first night in the two rooms that were her new home. All was sublimely peaceful and quiet. If there was a ghost in the house who came, like Wolf, on an inspection, Susannah neither saw nor heard nor felt it. She slept well, without so much as a disturbing dream.

The next morning Susannah put on her running clothes and drove to her father's house. She left her car in his driveway and proceeded to run for three miles along her usual route. Then she went into the house, greeted Sarah, drank a glass of juice, and asked how her father was this morning. Sarah replied that the Judge was sleeping late.

Ever since parking in the driveway, Susannah's old unreasonable guilt feelings had been bothering her. No matter what the Judge said, no matter how much he pushed her away, Susannah didn't want her father to think she was abandoning him. With that guilt like a rock in her side, she walked slowly down the hallway to the master bedroom and pushed open the door. She saw her father's long form on one side of the bed, the side he'd always slept on. The fact that he still left room for the wife who was no longer there tugged at Susannah's heart. She tiptoed in, telling herself she would just make sure he was all right. Which was silly—of course he was all right, he was only sleeping.

The Judge lay on his back, arms straight down at his sides. His eyes were closed, and his face looked ashen. The prescription bottle of antidepressants was on the bedside table, Susannah was glad to see. She'd been afraid he wasn't taking them. But—

But something was wrong. Suddenly Susannah couldn't breathe. Her eyes opened unnaturally wide. She stared at the Judge, watching with every nerve ending taut to the breaking point, for the slow rise and fall of his chest. And she saw nothing. Nothing!

*Oh, my God!* thought Susannah, gasping for air. She bent over and placed one hand on the Judge's chest. There was no movement, none at all, no breath of life there. She took his wrist between her fingers, but even before she felt for a pulse she knew it was too late, because his skin was cold. So cold. The Judge was dead.

Susannah placed her father's hand carefully back at his side. Her own heart was now thundering in her chest, and those taut nerve endings had begun to scream. She picked up the prescription bottle from the bedside table. It was far, far too light. He'd had forty-five tablets in this bottle, a six weeks' supply. She'd requested that amount herself, thinking that, if the antidepressant didn't kick in fully for a couple of weeks, it would probably take her a month beyond that to persuade the Judge to go for an evaluation. Now the bottle was completely empty. The conclusion was obvious.

Judge Harold Hathaway had overdosed on antidepressants. He had committed suicide.

## Chapter Eight

"It's my fault," said Susannah in a subdued, hollow voice. She was dry-eyed. Her face looked carved in stone.

"It's no one's fault," said Marvin Bradley, rubbing his chin as if he were pulling at a beard. "Not yours, or mine. I would have prescribed the same medication in the same quantity if he'd come to my office. You had no reason to think the Judge might be suicidal. Did you?"

Susannah shook her head. Talking was a tremendous effort. "I knew he was very unhappy. That's all." She stood up and began to pace aimlessly around her father's study. She'd called Dr. Bradley because it was necessary, and now she wanted him to leave. But he wouldn't, not until someone came to take the Judge's body away. She didn't want to be in this room, so permeated with her father's personality. But there was nowhere else in this house where she would be any more comfortable. She sat down again and linked her hands in her lap to keep them still.

"Ah, Susannah," said Marvin, still rubbing his chin, "the state medical examiner will have to be notified about this. You understand?"

She nodded.

"And under the circumstances... You do know that I was doing you a favor when I prescribed medication for your father without seeing him, don't you?"

Susannah nodded again, staring at him.

"Of course, the medical examiner probably won't call for any sort of an inquiry—this is clearly a suicide—but just in case... You wouldn't want me to get into trouble for doing you a favor, now would you?"

She tossed her hair out of her eyes and made the effort to speak. "What's your point, Marvin?"

"Why, only that I think it would be best, don't you, if I made, shall we say, an *adjustment* in my records. To make it look as if you brought the Judge in for a regular office visit, and *then* I prescribed the antidepressant for him. In case any questions are asked, that would be what you would say and what my records will show. That's all, it's really quite simple."

Susannah stared at him, slowly comprehending. She shook her head. "I won't lie, Marvin, and I don't want you to, either. If there are any questions, I'll take full responsibility. Like I said, this is my fault."

Marvin Bradley cast his pale, protuberant eyes up to the ceiling. "No, no, no, that attitude will never do! You may attempt to take responsibility, but I am the professional. The ultimate responsibility rests with me, and that's where the authorities would place it—if the medical examiner questions the cause of death. You must do as I say, Susannah. Really, your grief is clouding your judgment. I'll change the records, and you'll support me. Of course, it will never come to that, no questions will be asked. But just in case, you understand. Don't you?"

"Oh, all right. If it matters that much to you. As you say, you did do me a favor." She hung her head. "But I didn't do the Judge any favors. I might as well have killed him with my own hands."

Two men came with a collapsible cart, which they set up and wheeled down the hall to the master bedroom. Susannah showed them the way. She watched as they put the Judge's body on the cart, then she escorted them out the front door. She felt as if her body had suddenly become hollow inside, a shell without its living creature. She thought, *This is how a zombie must feel.*

Marvin put his arm around her shoulders. He said, "You shouldn't be alone at a time like this."

"I'm not alone. I have Sarah. And Tom."

"In that case—" he withdrew his arm "—I have patients to see. I'd better go."

"Goodbye," said Susannah automatically. "Thank you for coming." He left, and Susannah stood rooted at the study door.

Sarah Parrish came out of the kitchen. She fussed and clucked to no avail—Susannah could not be comforted. Like a robot, she got in her car and drove back to Laird's Mount. She did not speak to the workmen, or to Paul. She shut herself into her two rooms.

"SUSANNAH," SAID PAUL at the closed door "I know what happened. Tim heard it on the radio, on the local station. I respect your privacy, but I want you to open the door and let me in!" She made no response. Paul was nearly frantic. As soon as Tim had told him, he'd sent the work crew home so that Susannah could have peace and quiet. But he wasn't going to leave until he'd seen with his own eyes that Susannah was okay. How could she be okay? This was terrible!

He knocked again on the door, harder. "Susannah, please open this door. If you don't, I'm coming in anyway." He knew the door was merely closed, not locked, but still he hated to enter the room without permission. He thought, I'll count to ten. He counted silently. On six, the door opened.

Susannah's face was like a stark mask. Her wide gray eyes seemed flat, as if they were an opaque curtain closed against the world. She wore a long wool bathrobe in the dark green shade she liked. When she spoke, her tone was flat and automatic. "I don't want to talk. Go home, Paul."

He was confused. He didn't know what to do for her, but he wanted to do something. He ran his hand through his hair, messing it up, and took a step into the room. "I can't go home and leave you here like this. I just can't."

Susannah turned her back on him and walked slowly across the big room. It was cold. There was no fire in the fireplace, and her feet were bare.

"You need a fire in here. I'll make it," said Paul, watching her anxiously.

Susannah didn't respond, she merely returned to the chair she'd been sitting in and drew her feet up under her. She had furnished the room sparsely, with a double-bed mattress and box springs on a low metal frame against one wall, a couple of bookcases, a recliner with a floor lamp next to it near the fireplace, and in front of the windows, a long trestle table and two ladder-back chairs. She sat in one of these. There was a yellow legal pad on the table—she'd apparently been writing. So, at least she was doing something; that had to be better than nothing.

While Paul busied himself with the fire, he cast oblique glances Susannah's way. She didn't return to whatever she was writing. She seemed to be staring out the window. When the fire was blazing and he was satisfied that it would burn for a while, Paul went and sat in the other chair.

"What else can I do for you?" he asked.

"Nothing. I have everything I need."

Paul rubbed at his hair again. "You don't have a telephone here. There must be people I can call for you. Let me do that, at least."

"I'll take care of it myself, tomorrow, from the Judge's house. I made a list." She touched the yellow pad, and Paul looked at it. Columns of neat writing, everything numbered. She repeated, "You can go home now."

"No, no I can't. Not yet. I don't really think you ought to be alone tonight, Susannah."

She turned those big, dull gray eyes on him. "I want to be alone," she insisted. Susannah seemed incapable of realizing that she was acting exactly the way she'd described the Judge acting, insisting on being alone. She'd been concerned about him; Paul was concerned about her. But should he leave her alone, if that was really what she wanted, or should he try to make her come out of it?

He decided to try. He ached to touch her, to pull her into his arms, to caress and comfort her, but she seemed so remote, unapproachable. Paul leaned forward, elbows on his thighs, hands dangling emptily. "You should talk about it, at least. The radio report said Judge Hathaway committed suicide. How did it happen, Susannah?"

"I don't *want* to talk about it."

"I'm sure it's not healthy for you to keep everything locked up inside you like this. Come on, Susannah, please!"

"I can't believe they would put it on the radio."

Well, at least it was a beginning. "This is a small town, and the Judge was an eminent citizen, even if he had been here only a couple of years. They didn't give any details, it was just a simple statement."

Susannah did not respond. Except for the crackling of the fire, there was utter silence in the house. Paul felt the silence, an almost palpable hush. In a couple of hours it would be dark. This whole house with its high ceilings and large empty rooms would be black as the night outside—except for these two rooms of Susannah's. The silence and the darkness would surround her, press in on her. How in God's name could he go off and leave her in this place with her thoughts of death? And she *would* be thinking of death, Paul was sure of it.

When his sister had died of leukemia, the whole family—including grandmothers and grandfathers and aunts and uncles and cousins—had gathered at his house. And when his father's father had died, it was the same, they all went to be with his grandmother. This was not right, Susannah should not have to be so alone. Paul's voice sounded loud in his ears when he broke the silence. "Aren't there any relatives who would come and stay with you?"

She said matter-of-factly, without a trace of self-pity, "The Judge had Jane. Jane had the Judge. There is no other family. Perhaps that seems odd to you. It did to me, once. But that's the way it is, the way it has always been. The Judge and Jane had each other. I suppose that's why when she died he didn't want to go on living. Maybe there's life after death, maybe they're together again. This morning I thought I'd killed him, but now I don't because it was what he wanted. Now I think I set him free."

"What do you mean, you thought you'd killed him?"

"He overdosed on the antidepressants I got for him."

"God, what a shock that must have been for you!"

"I'm over it now. I'm fine. Go home, Paul. Wolf will be waiting for you."

Paul considered this. She did not look fine. She was entirely too composed—her face looked as if it had been carved from marble. He knew she'd be better if she could cry, as she'd cried in his arms the other night. "Have you cried yet, Susannah?"

"No."

"You need to cry. Hell, you need to yell and scream if you feel like it. That's the beginning of healing, to let the feelings out. Don't keep them all bottled up. Remember the other night? You said you felt better—"

"I remember. I made a fool of myself with you, and I don't intend to let it happen again. For any reason." Susannah stood up slowly, regally. "Good night, Paul."

She thought she'd made a fool of herself? Paul lumbered awkwardly to his feet, stunned by what Susannah had said. He felt as if she'd just dropped a rock into his chest, somewhere in the vicinity of his heart, and it was sinking to his feet, tearing his guts out on the way down. He made it to the doorway where he turned and looked back at the woman he loved, standing so proud and tall and cold. Stubbornly he shook his head back and forth, knowing he was defeated but unwilling to give up. "I just—I still don't think you should be alone tonight."

"I have always been alone. I've learned to prefer it," said Susannah with utter finality.

SHE DID NOT WANT TO SLEEP. She lay in her bed and looked up at the strange shadows cast by the fire upon the ceiling high above her. The shadows were darkness moving against darkness. She looked at the uncurtained window and she saw utter black night. Deep, endless black, blacker than any night she had ever known before coming to Laird's Mount. Is death like this? A black, empty void?

She listened to the emptiness of the old house around her. All was stillness, silence. Not even a breath of wind outside, to push against the brick walls, to sigh and murmur at the windows. Susannah thought, *I am utterly alone.*

She moved. Sat up. Listened again, and heard nothing. Not even the creaks and groans that old houses are supposed to make. And yet, she felt ...*something.* Something that tugged at her and made her want to move. To walk. To walk through the house.

Susannah put on her robe. The floor was cold under her bare feet. She hunted for her slippers, found them and put them on. She did not have a flashlight; she'd meant to get one but had forgotten. There were candles, though, the emergency household kind—Paul had put them in the room next door, the room that served as a makeshift kitchen and one day soon would be a real kitchen. Susannah found the candles and a pack of matches, lit one and dripped wax into a saucer until there was enough to make the candle stand upright. Then she opened the door from the kitchen to the lateral hall.

Susannah held the candle high, listening again. The silence was so great that it felt tangible, heavy. It seemed like the sound of waiting. The Mount was waiting for her to move through its lonely rooms. Susannah began to walk. Her soft leather slippers laid

down a noiseless trail behind her. Her candle cast a
lambent light and threw her shadow, huge and waver-
ing, upon the walls. As she traversed the hall, a
thought flickered into her brain. *Tonight I am claim-
ing Laird's Mount as my own.*

The stairs creaked when she climbed them. Her eyes
seemed able to see through darkness, and her mind
erased the clutter of work in progress as if it had not
been there at all. She moved from room to room, silently filling the old house with her presence.

Outside, a full moon emerged through a break in the
clouds and shed its light down, down upon Laird's
Mount. Down through the naked branches of the old
pecan trees, into the tall windows. The moonlight
made a pale rectangle upon the wide floorboards of
the upstairs hall, and in that light, shimmering motes
shaped themselves into the outline of a human form.
As Susannah emerged from a room with her candle
held out before her, she saw the pale rectangle and,
within it, a small explosion of shimmering specks that
swirled and then were gone. She raised the candle
high, and as she did the moon went behind clouds
again. The moonlight winked out, leaving behind it
total darkness. Her lips formed a soundless question:
*Mother?*

She sank down on the floor where the moonlight
had been. She put the candle down beside her, grasped
her knees and hugged them to her chest. She rested her
forehead on her knees and her hair fell forward like a
curtain hiding her face. Susannah did not see a large
black shape that loomed on the small stairway to the

third floor, but she felt its effect: a consuming, over-whelming sense of hopelessness and utter sorrow. She accepted the sorrow as her own. She wept.

The black shape, as if satisfied, dissolved into the darkness that surrounded it.

"NO, THANK YOU. I don't need a local lawyer, I'm continuing on with the same firm that has handled my father's business for many years. They're familiar with the laws of this state. There's no reason for us to talk further, so goodbye!" Susannah tossed her head. It was all she could do not to slam the telephone into its cradle. In the month since the Judge's death and bur-ial, more lawyers and stockbrokers and Realtors than she could count had called, soliciting her business un-der the thin guise of helpfulness and sympathy. Word got around fast that Susannah Hathaway was an heir-ess twice-over, a distinction she preferred to ignore.

She'd listed her father's house with Charles Her-bert, who had assured her of a quick sale. She'd gone through and tagged the pieces of furniture that she intended to keep and move to Laird's Mount—the rest she'd turned over to an antiques and used-furniture appraiser to be sold at an auction. She'd hounded the telephone company until they'd installed a telephone for her at Laird's Mount. She'd sold the Judge's black Lincoln. She'd promised Tom and Sarah Parrish that there would be work for them both at Laird's Mount soon. Keeping busy was good therapy and it worked—in the daytime. The nights were hard, but Susannah would not admit it. Especially to Paul Starbuck. At night, awake or asleep, sadness overwhelmed her. Hard as that was, it was better than feeling like an empty shell.

By day, Paul was something of a pest. Here he was rapping on the doorframe, then coming into her two-room domain with an armload of—

"What is that load of stuff you're bringing in here?" asked Susannah suspiciously. He'd appeared the moment she hung up the phone.

Paul grinned as he marched over to the table and deposited the items in question. "These are samples. Venetian blinds, authentic to the period. I want you to look at them and choose what you like. I've already got the windows measured and talked to the installer. Soon as we know which style, he'll get on out here and get the job done. This room first. You've lived here without the windows covered for long enough, Susannah."

"We ought to get the walls painted first," said Susannah stubbornly. "I already told you, I don't need curtains or anything out here. There's not another soul around for acres and acres, so who's to see? I could walk around naked at night, and nobody would ever know!"

Paul ignored her. He'd learned that there was no sense trying to reason with Susannah. If you wanted something done for her own good, you just had to go ahead and get started on it. "I had a paint analysis done on the walls and woodwork. If we want to go back to the original—and we do, right?" Susannah nodded. "Then we go with white woodwork and paneling in these downstairs rooms." He reached in his pocket and drew out a handful of small colored squares on a metal ring. "Of course, there are about a jillion shades of white—this one matches what was here originally."

He had caught Susannah's interest. She moved over to the table and took the ring of sample colors in her hand, flipped through them and began to ask questions. "What's this yellow?"

"That's the wall in the room west of this one. It may have been a music room."

"It's a nice color. I like it," said Susannah, "but how do you know it was a music room?"

"That came out of Jane's research."

"Oh." This information disturbed Susannah, but for the moment she wasn't sure why. "And this?"

It was a lovely muted rose color. "That's what we found, under two layers of wallpaper and several layers of paint, as the original shade in this room. This was either the parlor or a library. Your other room here, the future kitchen, was originally a kind of keeping room—that means they brought food into there from the separate kitchen outside, kept it warm and served from there. What we don't know is whether they served to the room on the right, or on the left. In other words—" Paul fingered through the samples in Susannah's hand "—this blue could have been the dining room. Whatever, it goes in the east room that corresponds to the music room on the west. And in all those rooms, the woodwork was this shade of white, here."

"Then I guess the blinds should be that same shade. That's simple enough." Susannah began to poke through the pile of slats that Paul had deposited on the table with a look of consternation. "The width of the slats is unusually wide, isn't it? And how far apart the cords are. They all look clunky. I guess I've gotten used to miniblinds. You're sure any one of these will be authentic?"

"Absolutely."

Susannah made a choice, then took it to the deep window embrasure. She held it up, squinting in the bright sunshine that poured through the window. She'd visited enough old houses, and also seen enough pictures of their interiors, to know that venetian blinds—no matter how modern an invention they seemed—had been widely in use in the seventeenth century.

She whipped around, knowing now what had disturbed her. "Paul, are you sure my mother didn't give her research papers to you?"

"You didn't find them among her things?"

"No, I never did. And after the Judge's death, I went through *everything.*"

"That's odd." Paul scratched his head thoughtfully, then shrugged. "But I guess it doesn't make much difference, since she told me about the parts that pertained directly to the restoration process. The rest was just who built it—and you found that out yourself—and who'd lived here when. That kind of thing. We don't really need Jane's papers. I wouldn't worry about it, if I were you."

Susannah wordlessly handed her choice for the blinds to Paul. Could he be concealing something from her behind that cheerful facade? Could the Judge actually have seen an intruder going through Jane's desk, or had that been, as Susannah had persuaded herself, a dream? Or a waking hallucination?

Paul tucked the chosen blind sample under his arm, repocketed the ring of paint squares, and was talking about something as he gathered up the rest of the blinds from the table. Susannah wasn't listening. She was gripped by an eerie feeling that someone in Kinloch hadn't wanted her to know whatever it was that Jane had found out about Laird's Mount. She was suddenly convinced that someone hadn't wanted Jane Hathaway in this house, and therefore, must not want Susannah here, either. It was high time that she tackled this problem—surely nothing else could happen to distract her from it! Unless she allowed herself to be distracted by somebody like Paul.

"You're not listening to me, are you?" Paul looked amused rather than annoyed.

"Sorry. What did you say?"

"I said, after the lunch break we should look over the outbuildings. The work inside the house is winding down, Susannah. We'll finish ahead of schedule. I'm ready to assign a couple of my men to pulling down and hauling off those ramshackle outbuildings so that I can call in the landscape architect. You ought to go through them with me, make sure there's nothing you want to keep."

"All right. I think we'll want to keep that brick dependency. I'll get to it soon, I promise."

PAUL WAS RELIEVED that Susannah didn't put up a fuss about doing away with the outbuildings. He thought the brick building, authentic dependency or not, should go, too. Maybe he'd be able to persuade her when it was time to do the demolition work.

Paul had been keeping a close eye on Susannah. As close as she'd let him get anyway. Just about every day when he and the men finished work, he asked her if she'd like to come to his house for supper, and she always refused. He kept asking because he suspected she wasn't eating much—she was naturally lanky, but lately her lankiness had a bony quality he didn't remember seeing before. He suspected she wasn't sleeping well, either, because of the dark circles under her eyes. And while that could be natural, considering that she'd lost both her mother and her father within a three-month period, still Paul wondered...

He wondered what Susannah did at night, all alone in that big old house. He wondered if she wandered around, and if so, was she awake or sleepwalking? He wondered this because he had begun to find that in the mornings things were not always where he knew he had left them at the end of the day. It was never anything very momentous, just a sawhorse moved, a rope untied, an extension cord in the wrong place, that kind of thing....

He hoped Susannah was doing it, even if that meant she was walking in her sleep. Because if she wasn't moving these things herself, *someone* was. Kinloch was virtually a crime-free town, but a woman alone in an isolated house could be a powerful enticement—to peepers, if nothing else. Paul could see that the windows were covered. He could get rid of outbuildings so that there would be no place to hide. He could repair the big iron gate and tell Susannah to keep it locked, but that wouldn't do much good—the gate had apparently been built for show, since there was no fence except for the cypress trees that made a kind of psychological barrier around the property. He could put in some outside lighting, but that would be expensive and couldn't be done without her approval.

There was only one other thing he could think of to do. He could come over and guard Laird's Mount himself.

# Chapter Nine

Susannah heard someone pounding on the front door of Laird's Mount. She was annoyed, assuming that Paul had forgotten something. She always looked forward to the end of the day, when she had a quiet house and the privacy to take a shower. In fact, she had already begun to get undressed.

The pounding came again. With a sigh of resignation, Susannah pulled her jeans back on and zipped them, crossed the lateral hall and jerked open the door. She blinked in surprise. It wasn't Paul, after all.

"Charles Herbert! What brings you out here?"

"Hey, Susannah. I was more or less in the neighborhood and decided I'd drop in. See how you're getting along. I hope you don't mind."

"I guess not. I'm a little grubby. I do a fair amount of the work here myself, along with the crew. But come in." She stepped back, out of the doorway. "I'm not exactly set up for entertaining, but I could offer you a soda."

Charles craned his thick neck, looking up at the

freshly plastered hall ceiling. "Nix on the soda. Say, you've really done a lot. How about a house tour?"

Susannah turned back, suddenly feeling possessive. She was reluctant to show her exquisite house to this acquisitive man, but she didn't have a good reason not to. "Well, okay."

He flashed his version of a winning smile—it consisted mostly of a lot of unnaturally white teeth. "Tell you what. I'll show myself around while you get cleaned up. Then I'll take you out to dinner. I have news about your other house, I'll tell you while we eat. What do you say?"

"No, thank you. I don't feel like going out tonight. But I will show you the house." Gritting her teeth, Susannah began to give her first house tour. She explained that the downstairs rooms were now completely finished, needing only a coat of paint on the walls and the floors sanded. "We're going to hand-sand them. No machines on this heart pine."

In the so-called music room, where Susannah planned to have a formal living room, Charles pointed a stubby finger upward. "Those whaddayacall-ums—"

"Cornices," Susannah guessed from the direction he pointed.

"Yeah. Those are great. Unusual, aren't they?"

"I believe the pattern is, yes. It's a variation on the scallop, with spoon-shaped indentations."

Charles nodded wisely. He commented on the carving of the fireplace surround, on the identical small porches being constructed outside the back doors of the west and east rooms. He remarked on the excellent condition of the wood in the balustrades and handrail of the large staircase.

"You seem to know this house rather well, Charles," Susannah observed.

"Yeah. I've been in here before. With Jane, I mean. Didn't look anywhere near this good, but I could see the potential, you know?"

They reached the second-floor hall, and Susannah halted. For some reason, she was apprehensive about bringing him up here. But that had to be nonsense. She gave an unconscious shrug and continued to play tour guide. "The ceilings here on the second floor are unusually high, fourteen feet, which is one foot higher than on the first floor. This large, square hall is unusual, too. We're still working on the rooms up here. Someone, I guess one of the Richardsons—" she looked over her shoulder to see if Charles reacted to the name; he didn't "—had put a bathroom up in one corner of this large bedroom, and when Paul tore it out, it left a pretty big mess."

Susannah went on to explain how she would have two new bathrooms in the gabled space over the east and west rooms. Charles seemed properly impressed, even if he did view it all with an envious gleam in his eye. When they returned again to the square hall, he stopped short, stuck his hands in his pockets and nervously rolled his eyes.

"What about up there?" He jerked his head in the direction of the stairs to the third floor.

"Interesting that you should mention it," said Susannah, "because I was just up there today for the first time. It's a mess, a huge jumble of junk has been dumped up there, probably by everyone who ever lived here. But there's something fascinating about that third floor."

"Yeah, I'll say," Charles muttered, cutting his eyes to the stairs and back.

"Probably because that space hasn't been lived in for such a long time—although right now it's filthy—it's actually in very good condition. The walls are intact, and under the grime the woodwork still has its original coat of paint—according to Paul. There are three rooms. I intend to do any repair work up there myself, once we've cleaned the junk out. There won't be much to do, and I think I may use it for a studio and office space for myself."

"Ah—" said Charles, backing away toward the main stairs. "I don't think you want to do that. No, I surely don't!"

"Why?"

"If you don't know, I don't think I should be the one to tell you. Let's go back downstairs now, okay? I'll give you my news and then I'll just be on my way. Unless—" he pulled a handkerchief out of his pocket and mopped his brow, which had started dripping in a nervous sweat "—you want to change your mind about going out to dinner."

Susannah was within an inch of agreeing to have dinner with him. Maybe, if she did, she could wheedle out of him whatever it was that made him so nervous about the third floor. Then again, maybe she could get it out of him without enduring the dinner—she'd just remembered that Paul had left a six-pack of beer in the refrigerator.

"We'll talk in my room, Charles. If you don't want a cola, maybe you'd prefer a beer?" Susannah smiled, determined to be exceptionally nice.

He accepted the beer, refused a glass, and guzzled about half of it straight from the can. Only then did he begin to visibly relax. The news he had to relate was an offer on the Judge's house. They discussed it, and Susannah made a counteroffer. She wanted to get that house off her hands, but not so far below her asking price.

"Very astute," said Charles, nodding his big head.

"I'm glad you think so. Would you like another beer?"

"You gonna relent and have dinner with me?"

"That depends," said Susannah sweetly. "Even if I do, you'll be here awhile longer, so how about that beer?"

"Don't mind if I do." He folded his hands on his stomach and tipped the ladder-back chair onto its back legs. "Know what you oughta do, Susannah?" he called after her.

She could hear him well enough—he had a voice that wouldn't have shamed a tobacco auctioneer. She raised her own voice from inside the pantry. "No, what?"

"You oughta let me put the Mount on the market now. You've got it almost completely done, and you could sell it before you go to the expense of furnishing it. I could get a pretty penny for this, I'll tell you, a pretty penny!''

Susannah handed Charles his second beer, though she felt like knocking him on the head with it. "Don't you ever give up?"

"Nope. That's the key to my success. I'm stubborn as an old mule, twice as pretty, and three times as smart. Come on, Susannah, you don't really want to live in this house for long, so why not get rid of it now? Our biggest selling season has already started, and all them Yankees will just be pouring down here looking for a place to retire in."

"Oh, but I do want to live in this house. Probably for a long, long time. I like it here."

"I thought you were just in Kinloch to help your daddy out. None of us thought you ever meant to stay on permanent. I mean, you got a career and all to think about."

"I can be an architect here, just as well as anywhere else. I'm becoming very interested in restoration, and there could be a lot of work in this part of the country for a good restoration architect. No—" she shook her head and set her lips in a firm line "—I'm definitely not going to put Laird's Mount up for sale. You can just forget it."

Charles Herbert swigged, wiped his mouth with the back of his hand and looked at Susannah with an uncertain expression on his beefy face. "I'll bet if I tell you about that third floor, you'll change your mind."

This was what Susannah wanted to know. Good! Now she'd find out for the price of two beers, Paul's beers at that—a heck of a lot cheaper than dinner. She said, "I'm listening."

Charles tipped his chair forward and leaned toward Susannah, resting his elbows on his thighs. "You ever have any, uh, strange experiences since you moved into this house, Susannah?"

She thought about the long, long nights, and the sadness, and how in the hours of sleeplessness she sometimes lost track of time. But she shook her head in denial. "Exactly what kind of strange experiences did you have in mind, Charles?"

"Ever hear anything? Ever see anything that, uh, shouldn't have been there?"

"You said you'd been here a lot with my mother. Did you or Jane ever hear or see anything?"

Charles looked away from Susannah. Beads of sweat popped out on his forehead again. "Well, yeah, I did." He looked at her again, and there was fear in his eyes. "I'm pretty sure I saw a ghost."

Although she didn't believe in ghosts, Charles Herbert's facial expression was convincing. Gooseflesh rose on Susannah's arms. She kept her voice level. "What did this ghost look like?"

"It was weird!" Charles fumbled for his handkerchief and mopped his forehead again. "You know you hear about ghosts being kind of white, maybe transparent? This wasn't like that, it was *worse* than that. This was a big black shape. I mean the thing was huge! It was like a kind of moving shadow, only there wasn't anybody there for it to be a shadow of. There was kind of a big head and shoulders and the rest was just a black mass."

Susannah believed him. She didn't want to, but she did. "When was this? And where were you when you saw it?"

"It was when I first heard the Richardson family might be willing to sell the Mount. I brought Jane out here because I knew she'd been riding around the countryside looking at old houses. She was active with the preservation society and all that, and I thought she'd want to see it. Hell, we didn't even need a key to get in, the place was so neglected. It was late in the afternoon, so it was kind of dark in here, and we were up on the second floor. I was out in the hall, waiting for her to quit poking around in one of the bedrooms, and I got this really weird feeling. I don't know how to describe it, but it sure wasn't good. I started looking around kind of nervouslike, and that's when I saw it. The damn thing came moving down that little staircase that goes up to the third floor. Big black shape, just floating down. I nearly peed my britches!"

"You're sure it couldn't have been a person, and it was just too dark for you to see clearly? I mean, you thought you and Jane were alone in the house, so seeing someone else would have been a shock. And you did say that the door was unlocked, anyone could have gotten in. Maybe your eyes were playing tricks on you."

Charles shook his big head back and forth emphatically. "No way. That thing maybe didn't look like I've heard ghosts are supposed to look, but that's what it was, all right! Because I was too damn scared to move. I just stared at it. And I swear to God, Susannah, right while I was looking at it the damn thing disappeared!''

"Did Jane also see this ghost?''

"No, like I said she was in one of the bedrooms. After the thing disappeared I yelled at her to come on, it was time to leave.''

"Did you tell her about it?''

"Are you kidding? A fragile little lady like your mother? No way. I just rushed her out of there and made some excuse like I had another appointment or something.''

Susannah was quiet, thinking. Charles seemed relieved to have told his story. He tossed down the last of his beer. At last she said, "You let my mother buy this house, knowing that there was something in here that had scared you half to death.'' Her choice of words was deliberate.

"Hey, she was dead set on it. Had to have it. And besides, I'd just about convinced myself I hadn't seen anything.'' He tugged at his collar. "I'll tell you though, Susannah, when Jane died like that, I felt guilty that I hadn't told her. You know? So...well, I've told you. And you know what? I feel better for it. *Now* will you let me put this place on the market?''

The man disgusted Susannah. On the one hand, he felt a duty to tell her about this supposed ghost, yet on the other hand he was perfectly willing to sell the house, ghost and all, to some unsuspecting stranger!

Still, she wasn't quite through with him yet. "Marvin Bradley told me something that might interest you."

"Yeah? What?"

"He apparently knows about the ghost, too. He said his opinion was that my mother saw it, and it frightened her so much that she went into cardiac arrest."

Charles Herbert tugged at his collar again. "That's, uh, kind of hard to believe."

"What's just as hard for me to believe is that in spite of his opinion on the cause of Jane's death, Marvin Bradley still wants to buy Laird's Mount himself. Do you think that's a little peculiar, Charles?"

"If you ask me, the Doc's a little peculiar, period. Hell, if he wanted it, I'd sell it to him in a heartbeat."

"I'm sure you would," said Susannah acerbically. She stood up, ready to dismiss him. "Charles, I appreciate you telling me what you saw, and your inviting me to dinner. I really am tired and I don't want to go anywhere tonight. But I have one last question before you leave."

Charles heaved to his feet and waited for Susannah to ask her question.

"Were you here, secretly, at Laird's Mount with Jane the afternoon of her death?"

"What are you getting at, Susannah? Everybody knows she was alone when it happened."

"I don't think she was. Just answer the question, please."

"No, I most definitely was not! I didn't go around having secret meetings with Jane Hathaway. Maybe I would have liked to, but I didn't. If anybody met her

out here that day before her appointment with Starbuck, it sure as hell wasn't me!''

His denial was too fervent to be convincing.

THE ACRES OF LAWN sloping down behind Laird's
Mount were the bright green of new grass, liberally
sprinkled with yellow dots of blooming daffodils.
Spring had come to the Virginia Piedmont region. The
air held a kind of freshness that tugs at the heartstrings.

Or perhaps it was Paul Starbuck who tugged at Susannah's heartstrings, no matter how hard she tried to
armor herself against him. He stood a few feet ahead
of her, his hands thrust in the pockets of his jeans and
his feet widely planted. A light breeze ruffled his curly
black hair. He said, ''God, this is beautiful!''

''Yes, it is,'' Susannah agreed while she tried to
strengthen her emotional armor, ''but the view is not
why we came out here. Let's get going, Paul.''

He looked back over his shoulder and quipped,
''All work and no play—''

''Makes Susannah a very productive woman.'' She
strode across the grass toward the falling-down
wooden building near which their various cars and
trucks were parked. When he'd caught up, she waved
her hand at it. ''I think this whole thing has to go—
there's nothing worth saving here. Is there? Do we
need to go through it?''

''I've already done that. I agree, it has to come
down. I'll put one of the men right on it.''

Susannah couldn't resist a little poking around. "I guess this was a carriage house. And there must have been stables for the horses."

"Watch yourself, don't step on a rusty nail or something. Have you had a tetanus shot recently?"

"You're not my keeper, Paul," said Susannah crossly. And then she mentally stopped short. Inside her head she could hear her father's voice, saying exactly the same thing to her. In a single flash of insight, she understood. For weeks, she'd been repeating the Judge's pattern, as if it had been handed down as genetically as her bone structure. As if, now that he was gone, she had an obligation to be more like him than ever. Well, that would have to stop, right now!

Because of his height, Paul ducked his head as he made his way inside the ramshackle building to join Susannah. He put his hands back in his pockets and said seriously, "I might like to be your keeper, Susannah. Sometimes I think you could use one."

Sunshine fell through holes in the roof and highlighted the broad planes of Paul's face—such a strong face, yet at the same time so sensitive. The sensitivity was in his dark-lashed eyes and in the curves of his mouth, but more than that, it radiated from him to her. "I just realized," Susannah confessed, "that I haven't been very nice to you since my father died. You've been so caring, and I've kept shutting you out. I'm sorry, Paul. I'll try not to do that anymore. I, of all people, know how it feels to be shut out."

"I do care about you, you know."

Susannah hung her head. She could feel her armor dissolving. "I know."

He moved close. "Susannah—"

Strong, work-toughened fingers cupped her chin and raised her face to his. Her heart, already tugged by the softness of spring, opened up. She closed her eyes, knowing that he would kiss her.

Paul's kiss was gentle. He wrapped her in his arms and murmured into her hair, "I care about you a lot." The broad expanse of his chest heaved with a sigh. "I've gone nuts worrying about you. And I was afraid I'd never have another chance to hold you like this again. Thank you—thank God!—for coming back to me."

Susannah pulled back so that she could look into Paul's eyes. "I haven't been gone anywhere. I'm just not very good at being close. And you are. Being close isn't hard for you, but it is for me."

Paul ran his hands down Susannah's arms, then took her hands in his and brought them to his lips. Somehow it was the perfect thing to do. He said, "I do understand. I've had a lot of time to think. In a way, I took advantage of you that night you came to my house, but I didn't mean to. I thought—" For a moment Paul frowned, and Susannah wanted to reach up and wipe the frown away. But he still held her hands tightly; she could feel in that grip the intensity of his search for the right words. "I thought you needed me—" the frown smoothed away and Paul's dark blue eyes blazed with naked emotion "—and I knew that I needed, I *wanted* you."

"I—"

Paul placed a finger on Susannah's lips. "You don't have to say anything. I've learned something about you since then. I have the greatest respect for you, Susannah. I've seen how you handled yourself in a situation that was more awful for you than I can imagine. I know now that you don't *need* me. You don't need anyone, you're a survivor and you can take care of yourself. But I hope that some day you may want me, as I still want you."

Susannah nodded, thrilled yet stunned by his words. Too stunned to make a response. Paul seemed to know her, and to expect nothing from her. He made what might have been an awkward moment easy, by tucking her to his side, turning and marching them both out of the old carriage house.

When they were outside once more he let her go and grinned, saying, "In the meantime, as you pointed out, we have lots of work to do. I was going to tell you—the old stables were down by that pond, you know where it is, hidden by high grass down and to the east of the slope."

"I know where you mean, I saw it when I was looking for the family graveyard, which is not too far from the pond."

"There was also a kind of shack down there—God knows what its purpose was, but it looked like some homeless person had been living there in the not-too-distant past. I didn't think that was such a good idea, so I tore down the shack, and the stables, too, right after Jane hired me. When the landscape guy gets going here, you ought to have him clean up the pond. It could be an asset."

"I will. Now, let's go look at that little brick building." As Paul and Susannah walked the short distance to the brick dependency, Wolf came bounding up. Laughing, Susannah accepted the dog's enthusiastic greeting. "I didn't know you brought Wolf with you today!"

"I hope you don't mind. It's such a gorgeous day and I thought Wolf could do with a run."

"Wolf is welcome here anytime." Susannah broke stride to pet her, and got a lick on the cheek in return.

"Why don't you let me get you a dog, Susannah?"

Instantly she was wary. "Oh, I don't know. I like Wolf, and I trust her because she's your dog. But I don't know enough about them to have one of my own."

Paul didn't push it.

Susannah entered the small brick building. Inside it was damp, cool and dark. Soot-blackened windows were small and high up, not intended for light but only for ventilation. The single room was larger than it appeared from the outside, a rectangle about fifteen-by-twenty feet. It was completely empty, which was a surprise considering the clutter that had greeted Susannah in every other part of the property. As her eyes grew accustomed to the dim light, she saw that one wall was almost completely taken up by a huge brick fireplace.

"How odd," she remarked, "there's that huge fireplace, but I never noticed a chimney on this building."

"I expect it crumbled away a long time ago. The remnants are probably up there on the roof. You could see them if you tried from any of the upstairs windows in the house."

"Mmm," Susannah agreed. She went up to the fireplace and inspected it closely. "I've never been in one of the old kitchen dependencies—I don't know what it's supposed to look like."

Wolf came in, her nails clicking softly on the old floorboards. Neither Paul nor Susannah paid any attention to her.

Paul came alongside. "That's what it was, all right. A kitchen. See here—" he pointed to two large holes in the bricks to the right of the vast fireplace opening "—those are the ovens. Their doors are long gone, but I expect with a bit of work we could reproduce them. That is, unless you'll agree to let me pull this down, too. You're not making a showplace out of Laird's Mount, Susannah. Why keep this building? It's not particularly interesting architecturally, and it could turn into a hazard."

She was walking slowly around the perimeter of the room. Wolf, nose down, was sniffing at the floor in the center. Susannah asked, "What do you mean, a hazard?"

Paul ruffled the back of his hair. "Oh, like that old shack I pulled down before. We don't get many homeless people around here, but there are always drifters looking for a place to camp out for a night or two. A little building like this, with the roof intact, it's kind of like an open invitation. I think you'd be wise to let me get rid of it for you."

"No, I like it. It's interesting. Maybe one day I'd like to do an authentic restoration. I could go over and look at the one Barbara Blair has, it might give me some ideas—"

Wolf growled and pawed at the floor; her nails made a scrabbling sound.

"What is it, girl," demanded Paul, his long legs taking him to the dog in two strides, "what have you found?"

The dog tossed her head, barking sharply. She clawed at the floor, growled ominously, and ran her nose along some invisible line.

Paul pushed the dog away, holding her back with his forearm. The other hand he ran along the floor, as the dog had done with her sensitive nose. "There's a trapdoor here. And from the way Wolf's behaving, I'd say there's something down there." He sounded grim. He turned to his dog and commanded, "Sit, Wolf!" Wolf was so excited by her discovery that he had to give the command a second time before she obeyed.

Susannah went down on her knees. In the dim light she had difficulty seeing what Paul was talking about. "Where?"

"Here. The ring is gone—you know, to open it by— but that wouldn't be a problem if someone wanted to get it open. A crowbar, any kind of prying tool would do it."

"Well, go get a crowbar then. And a flashlight. Let's see what's down there."

"No." Paul sank back on his haunches. "I know what this is, Susannah, I've seen them before. There's an old root cellar down there, and it's probably full of snakes. A whole nest of snakes."

Susannah cocked her head to one side, considering Paul. Wolf did the same. He did not look like a man who would be afraid of snakes, but in the dimness she could see an expression of—if not exactly fear—extreme wariness on his face. "I'm no herpetologist, Paul, but I think it's too early in the season for snakes to nest and produce baby snakes. If you won't get some sort of tool to open this trapdoor, then I will!"

"Okay, okay. We'll both go. I'll get a crowbar and you get a flashlight, and we'll leave Wolf in the house. Okay?"

Susannah agreed, though she argued that Wolf, having made the discovery, should not have to stay in the house. Paul relented.

But when they heaved up the trapdoor, amid much sniffing and growling from Wolf, they were disappointed. They had discovered nothing more than an old root cellar, carved long ago out of the earth, with an earthen floor and walls and one very well-preserved width of wood shelving. A ladder, which would have provided a way to climb down, lay on the packed earth where it must have fallen long ago.

Susannah, observing how Wolf pranced nervously and continued to growl, said lightly, "I think maybe we should get down there and start digging. The way Wolf is acting, you'd think we'd found buried treasure."

## Chapter Ten

After a long absence, the haunting dream returned. But now it was different. Now it had a nightmarish quality and seemed to go on and on, so that Susannah woke from it both frightened and exhausted. She dreamed it night after night. The good news was that if she was dreaming she must be sleeping more. The bad news was that Susannah still didn't know what her mother was trying to tell her.

The dream began in much the same way that it had before, with Jane's face zooming in, too terribly close, so that Susannah could see the anguish in her mother's eyes. But then it went on to another dimension, in which Susannah, led on, it seemed, by her mother's spirit, roamed ceaselessly from room to room. In this nightmare, Laird's Mount was not as it was in reality, a relatively small house with a few impressively large rooms. It became a dark, labyrinthine complex, an architectural maze, in which Susannah walked and walked, twisted and turned and lost her way. All the while she called, "Mother? Mother?" And in every dream she fought her way through this endless maze, in the end emerging in the same place—the upstairs hall.

Yet when Susannah really awakened, she would be in her own bed, in the room that was now her home. One morning, as she dragged herself out of bed, she noticed that the soles of her feet were dirty. She didn't think much of it since her habit was to go barefoot in her owm room at night, but she supposed that in the future she should try to remember to wash her feet before retiring.

PAUL STARBUCK HAD WASHED the day's dirt off in the shower, and now he was shaving and having a conversation with Wolf in the process. The dog's black-and-silver body filled the entire doorway of the bathroom, and her intelligent yellow eyes were fastened on her master.

"This is an important night, Wolf. Susannah has finally agreed to go out with me."

The dog cocked her head to one side, listening.

"I thought I'd take her someplace different—away from Kinloch. Edmister's Tavern." Paul rinsed the razor under the faucet and started on the left side of his face. He didn't like electric razors, not with his heavy beard.

Wolf panted and smiled, as if in approval.

"I don't think you'd like it." Paul turned and smiled over at the dog. "It's too crowded with people for your taste. The food's great, but the main thing is that on Friday and Saturday nights they have a country-and-western combo that starts playing about eight o'clock. And tonight's Friday. After we eat there'll be dancing.''

The dog gave an encouraging reply.

"Slow dancing. Two-step, fox trot, and all that."

Wolf made a noise deep in her throat, cocked her head to the other side, and her smile disappeared.

Paul paused and looked over at Wolf. "You couldn't possibly understand that word, *fox*. Anyway, it's not the kind of fox that would interest you. What do you think? Will Susannah dance with me?"

Wolf thumped her tail on the floor in lieu of barking. Then she decided she'd had enough of this conversation and walked away. Paul laughed. He was optimistic, feeling good. The soft spring weather had something to do with how he felt, but mostly it was because he thought he was making progress with Susannah. He had better be—with the restoration of Laird's Mount so close to completion, he was about to lose his opportunity to be near her every day.

He dressed casually, but well, in a white cotton turtleneck, gray trousers, and a navy blue sport coat that was only a little darker than his eyes. He tried to comb the curls out of his hair but soon gave it up as a lost cause. Humming tunelessly, he made sure Wolf had enough food and water to last for a few hours, grabbed his keys and locked the door.

On the short drive to Laird's Mount, Paul wished he could afford to have a nice car in addition to the truck he needed for his work. Sure, it was a great truck and all, but Susannah was used to better things. This led him to something he didn't like to think about—

Susannah's money. The talk around town was that she'd inherited a bundle from Jane, and then an even bigger bundle from the Judge. Who was he, Paul Starbuck, to be thinking about a woman who had so much money? He ought to be more realistic. The most he could hope for was that she'd let him get close to her for a time, and then she'd be moving on.

Paul scowled as he turned the truck between the mailboxes on St. Andrews Road and started up the gravel driveway. He didn't like thinking this way, and it sure as hell wasn't a good way to start off an evening that he'd been looking forward to for weeks!

There was a silver-gray car parked in the drive at the end of the walk. Not the white car that had been Jane's and was Susannah's now. Paul drove very slowly around to the side of the house, all the while keeping his gaze fastened on the front door. At the last moment before the front of the house disappeared from his view, Paul stepped on the brake. A man had emerged on the front entrance portico. Tallish, slim build, light-colored hair in a military-style cut. Not wanting to be caught staring, Paul stepped on the gas, sped around the corner to the parking area where they'd torn down the old carriage house, and slammed out of the truck.

He ran up the back steps on the east side and without thinking, pulled out and used his own key. He strode through the music room and found Susannah standing in the lateral hall outside the door of her room.

He demanded, "What was *he* doing here?"

"Good evening," said Susannah, "I see you let yourself in." She went into her room, ignoring his question.

Gripped by an unpleasant feeling that he didn't stop to identify as jealousy, Paul followed on Susannah's heels. "That was Doc Bradley, wasn't it?"

"Yes," said Susannah over her shoulder as she went from her big room into the smaller one, where the bathroom was, "and if you'll excuse me, his visit interrupted my dressing. Since you're already making yourself at home, please continue to do so. I'll be ready in a few minutes." And she shut the door in Paul's face.

Paul paced, his thoughts running a mile a minute. He didn't like Marvin Bradley—couldn't say exactly why, just didn't like him. Paul was never sick himself, but if he did happen to be some time in the future, he'd go all the way to Danville before he'd go to that creep! Was Susannah sick, was that why the doctor had been here? Nah. Doctors don't make house calls anymore. So he was seeing Susannah, hanging around Laird's Mount after Paul and his crew had gone for the day. Didn't even wait for an invitation, just felt free to come over any time. Which had to mean— didn't it?—that Susannah had been seeing a lot of the creep.

Paul had worked himself into a state by the time Susannah came back into the room. With his vision sensitized by jealousy, she looked more beautiful than he'd ever seen her. She'd done something to emphasize her eyes, there was a trace of pink along her

splendid cheekbones, and her shoulder-length hair
shone like antique gold. She wore a knockout purple
dress that he'd never seen before—the truth was, he
hardly ever saw Susannah in a dress—with a skirt that
flared and stopped a couple of inches above her knees.
It showed off her long, long legs. In heels. Not very
high heels, but they looked great.

Susannah put her hands on her hips and said, "You
know, Paul, one of these days you're going to have to
get used to the idea that this is my house. You really
shouldn't come barging in the back door like that
when I don't know you're here."

"You might be doing something you wouldn't want
me to interrupt, is that it?"

Susannah tossed her head. "I might."

"With Dr. Marvin Bradley?"

"Could be. Stranger things have happened."

"Have you been, uh, seeing him?"

"You might say that."

Paul felt like she'd kicked him in the stomach. "A
lot?"

Unexpectedly, Susannah laughed. He hadn't heard
her laugh like that in a long time. He liked the sound,
but it confused him. She said, "Maybe I never should
have agreed to go out socially with you, Paul. I didn't
know you were the possessive type."

"Possessive? I'm not possessive!"

Susannah walked by him, her chin in the air, to the
built-in cabinet beside the fireplace. The skirt of her
dress flipped around her legs in a way that was un-

bearably enticing to Paul. "You could have fooled me," she declared.

"I'm—I feel—" he floundered until he found the right word "—protective of you. I can't help it. And the Doc's a creep!"

Susannah closed the cabinet and turned to him with a purse in her hand. Her lips curved up, but not exactly in a smile, and there was a glint in her eye. "Maybe you'd rather I was *seeing* Charles Herbert?"

This was like waving a red flag at a bull. "Has he been after you, too?" Paul roared.

Laughing again, Susannah crossed to where Paul stood and placed her long fingers on his arm. The fake smile faded and her voice went soft. Her eyes went soft, too. "The truth is that I'm not really seeing either one of them. Not the way you mean. In Marvin Bradley's case, it's not that he hasn't tried. He comes over with the excuse that he's concerned about my health."

"Oh." Paul studied Susannah's face and saw how the circles under her eyes were still there, under a clever veil of makeup. "I guess I can't be too hard on him for that. I've been kind of concerned about your health, too."

She tossed her head again. "That's just his excuse. He doesn't really care about my health. He really is trying to develop some sort of a relationship with me."

"Is he getting anywhere?"

Mischievously, Susannah ran her hand up Paul's arm until she seized his shoulder and turned him toward the door. "That's enough questions. Now, are we going to this interesting place you promised me, or are we going to stand here all night talking about Marvin Bradley?''

EDMISTER'S TAVERN WAS out on an old country crossroads, about twenty minutes east of Kinloch. Paul couldn't get Marvin Bradley out of his head. He hated that, it was wrecking his precious time with Susannah, but he had to talk about the man some more.

"You don't really like him, do you? Bradley?" He'd gotten over the spurt of jealousy, so it came out less like a challenge and more like a simple request for information.

Susannah seemed to recognize the difference, but she looked over at him, as if to check, before answering. "Marvin's a complicated man, Paul. I can see why you'd call him a creep—sometimes he has a way of looking at you that is a little creepy. But there's a lot more to him than that. He's very intelligent, and believe it or not, he has a kind of charm that can be very... well, seductive."

"*Seductive?* Marvin Bradley?" Paul took his eyes off the road and looked at Susannah. Her lips were curved in a dreamy little way that he didn't like one bit.

She said, "Uh-huh. Another woman would understand, but I doubt a man would pick it up. Marvin has a kind of sensuality that's genderless. Or maybe it's androgynous. I expect that would be lost on anyone as masculine as you are."

"Hmm." Paul wanted to ask just how far the doctor's seduction had gone, but he didn't dare.

"Now, tell me about this place we're going—what's it called?"

"Edmister's Tavern." Paul told her about it, leaving out the part about the dancing, he wanted that to be a surprise. After several minutes of silence, he returned to the previous subject. Something about Marvin Bradley had been nagging at him, like an aching tooth. He couldn't leave it alone. "I think your mother felt the same about Dr. Bradley. Only maybe more so."

Susannah moved restlessly in her seat, but all she said was, "Oh?"

Paul removed one hand from the steering wheel and used it to rub at the back of his head. He decided to take another tack. "You haven't said much about it lately, but I get the feeling that you haven't given up on what you said you were going to do the first time I met you—try to find out more about the way Jane died."

"That's right. I've been working at it the only way I know how. I don't like to say this, but I do think someone was responsible for her death. It's not a rational thing, but a very strong conviction. Reinforced by these dreams I've been having."

"Want to tell me about the dreams?"

"No. They wouldn't make any sense to you. They just sort of . . . drive me on. Make me keep working at it. I think her death had a connection with Laird's Mount. For some reason, somebody either didn't want her to have the house, or didn't want her to find out much about it. I think her research papers were stolen, so I've been trying to reconstruct what she did. I went to the library, but that didn't get me very far. Then I thought of going to the preservation society. I found out they don't have an office."

"That's right." Paul signaled and turned left. He was only a few miles from the tavern now, and the conversation had become much more interesting. "They can't afford a headquarters. I know they keep hoping someone will donate an old house to them, but so far, no such luck."

"I called Barbara Blair. She's going to see me tomorrow. I intend to ask her if she knows what steps Jane took in her research." Susannah sighed. "I just hope she'll be willing to tell me. She didn't like my mother very much."

"I've wondered if I should tell you this, and now I think it's time. You mother could be a fairly disturbing person, Susannah. Especially to men. I always thought she was kind of innocent about it, she had that air about her, as if she didn't realize what she was doing. But if she went too far—well, there are people who wouldn't have liked her for it. Maybe she got in over her head, involved in something dangerous that we don't know about."

For a couple of miles Susannah said nothing, she was lost in her own, probably unhappy, thoughts. When she spoke again what she said shocked Paul right down to his toes. "Barbara told me enough that I had figured that out. The person who was most likely

to have been so incensed that he went beyond all reason was my father. Jane did the unthinkable—she
broke out of their exclusive two-person relationship,
and it must have driven him at least half-crazy. He
hated Laird's Mount, he actually said to me that the
house had taken Mother away from him. The Judge
was a criminal lawyer before he became a judge, and
then he sat on the criminal court. If anyone could plan
a crime that could be committed without detection, the
Judge could do it."

Paul clutched the steering wheel. The lights of Edmister's Tavern were ahead. He said grimly, "You
don't want to think that."

Susannah hung her head. "No, I don't. That's why
I keep on looking, pursuing the Laird's Mount connection. But so far the Judge is the only person who
fits the few clues I have. Mother's research papers are
gone, Paul, and the Judge told me there was an intruder in his house who must have stolen them. I
didn't want to believe him, it seemed too fantastic. I
decided he'd dreamed it, or had a hallucination. *Or* he
made that up. The Judge could easily have destroyed
those papers himself."

EDMISTER'S TAVERN HAD a kind of rustic, down-home
atmosphere that immediately put Susannah at ease.
The building was new, but it had been built on a site
where other taverns had stood for two hundred years.
In keeping with that long history, the present tavern
had been constructed in the style of a rambling old log
cabin. The curtains and tablecloths were green-and-

white gingham, and every table had a small oil lamp that burned with a golden flame. Everyone was casually dressed—she didn't see a single suit and tie in the place—but when she opened the menu Susannah realized that this couldn't be where the country folks hung out. Everything was ridiculously expensive.

She looked at Paul over the top of her menu. He must have known what she was thinking because he smiled and said, "I've been here lots of times before, and the food's worth it."

He was right. By the time she'd polished off a piece of rare roast beef that was more meat than she usually ate in a month, not to mention perfectly roasted potatoes and the best Caesar salad she'd ever had anywhere, Susannah had forgotten that there was anything more to life than good food, good wine and the most wonderfully comfortable company. She loved being with Paul. She liked simply looking at his face in the lamplight. She liked the way his hair curled a little around his ears and how one errant, curling lock flopped down onto his forehead. Most of all, she liked the sapphire glow in his eyes when he looked at her. It made her feel warm and limp all over. *Let's face it, he makes me feel loved.*

A three-piece combo, guitar, fiddle and bass, played old-time music, and a few couples danced on a small dance floor. When Paul stood up and held out his hand, Susannah flowed happily into his arms. His hand in the small of her back felt strong, he was easy to follow. Gradually he eased her closer, and closer, until his head was against her cheek and the length of his body pressed against hers. He was a very good dancer.

Susannah knew she was falling in love with Paul Starbuck. For once, she did not put up any barriers. She surrendered herself to the music and movement, the delicious luxury of being in Paul's arms. They fit together perfectly, their bodies melded smoothly in the slow rhythm of the dance.

"I knew it would be like this," Paul murmured in her ear. "We fit together, Susannah. We belong together, I can feel it. Can't you?"

She could, and in his arms she could not lie. "Yes," she whispered. Paul's lips caressed the curve of her ear, sending a shiver of delight down her spine.

THE MAGIC LASTED until they returned to Laird's Mount and Susannah asked Paul if he would like to come in. She didn't want the evening to be over, didn't want to lose that rare feeling of closeness, of being cherished.

Yet as soon as they stepped over the threshold, it disappeared. She became uneasy, told herself she should not have invited him inside, moved away too quickly and said too brightly, "I don't have the usual kind of nightcap, but there's beer and plain seltzer water."

With a brisk step Susannah started to cross the lateral hall to her room, where she'd left the door open and a light burning. Paul reached out, and caught her up in his arms. "I'm not thirsty, but I *am* hungry. For you." His mouth closed over hers.

Her body remembered Paul's kisses and began to respond on its own. Pleasure rippled along every nerve, a hot core of desire formed deep inside and began to radiate outward, sending signals to her most secret places. But Susannah's mind had become trapped in a cold place and would not obey.

Her mind triumphed. All her responses shut down. Susannah moved out of Paul's embrace and began walking backward along the path of light to her room. She couldn't speak, nor could she see the expression of pleading in her own eyes. Paul let his arms drop to his sides and, with a puzzled look on his face, followed her.

Susannah dropped her purse on the bed, then sat in one of the ladder-back chairs at the table. A shiver, sharply contrasting to the warmth of the night and to the warmth of Paul's arms, shook her relentlessly. She didn't know what was wrong. Only a few minutes ago she had wanted to be as close to Paul as two people can get, she'd wanted to make love with him here, in her own bed, in the house they had worked together to restore to life. A few minutes ago, nothing could have seemed more perfect, or more appropriate. But not now.

Paul sat in the other chair. Taking her hand, he asked, "What's wrong?"

She shook her head. "I don't know. I'm not sure."

"I read your signals wrong? No, I didn't—I'm sure I didn't. You changed your mind, then. I went too fast for you. I'm sorry, but Susannah, it's been so damn hard for me. Working here, sometimes right alongside you, day after day, and always knowing how much I want you..." He dropped her hand, pushed his chair back a foot, and stuck his own hands in his pockets. He looked away for a moment, took a deep breath, and when he turned back to her the look of troubled passion was gone from his face. Instead, he wore a friendly smile. "Hey, you know there's something I never told you?"

Susannah felt that she was hearing Paul from a great distance, yet she recognized the effort he was making and was grateful for it. She responded automatically, "What?"

"You're a good worker. I never expected someone like you—" he looked her up and down, thoroughly, and something passed like a shadow through his dark eyes "—to get down like a regular member of the crew. I guess I thought you'd be kind of a snob. Professionally, that is." Paul leaned forward again, reached out and took her hand once more, as if he were unable to keep himself from touching her. "We make a good team, Susannah. Professionally, as well as personally. I want you to remember that promise you made me not too long ago."

"Promise?" Susannah blinked, trying to bridge the vast distance that inexplicably yawned between herself and Paul.

"You promised you wouldn't shut me out."

Susannah blinked again. The distance was getting smaller, she was coming back. "I did say that. I remember."

"Good. But you were doing it again. Shutting me out."

"I won't do it anymore." She tried to smile. "Maybe we should go out the front door and come in again!" But even as she said it, she knew it was too late.

Paul caressed her fingers with his own fingertip. He turned her hand over, opened the palm and kissed it. Then looked into her eyes. "I have a different idea. Not necessarily better, but different. Why don't you figure out what just happened, and tell me. Was it just that I was coming on too strong, or was it something else?"

"Something else." Susannah reclaimed her hand and rubbed her forehead with it. "All the way home I didn't want our evening to end, I wanted to keep on feeling the way I felt when we were dancing. I wanted—I wanted even more than that. But as soon as we came through the front door..." She lost the thread of thought in the dark maze of her mind.

"Go on," Paul insisted.

Susannah closed her eyes, intensifying the darkness she felt inside. "It's this house. It wants something from me. It's like a compulsion, so huge that it blots out everything else." Her eyes flew open; her mouth dropped open, too.

"What is it, what's wrong?"

"It's *you!* How could I—!" She was for the moment unable to continue.

Paul gripped her hands tighter. "Go *on.*"

"Paul, I don't really know you. You seem so open, so completely guileless, it's hard to suspect you of being anything other than who you appear to be."

"Hey," Paul chuckled, but it sounded forced, "what you see is what you get!"

"I'm not so sure. I think it's time for you to tell me about you and Jane. Tell me *everything*."

"So that's it," Paul said quietly. He looked directly into Susannah's eyes. "I never lied to you about my feelings for your mother, Susannah. I liked her. Period."

"Barbara Blair implied there may have been more than that. She named you, Paul, as one of the men Mother may have been involved with."

"I don't get involved with clients. Except for you. You are the exception, Susannah. With you I haven't been able to stay uninvolved. You're too precious, too important to me. In the beginning, I tried to keep my distance, but I'm human. I'm almost unbearably attracted to you."

"We were talking about my mother."

Paul sighed, rubbed his head and put his hands in his pockets again. "All right. She came on to me a little. Well, that's not exactly right—she came on to me a lot. But only once, and when I didn't pick up on it she stopped. Nothing happened, nothing at all. I really believe that your mother was just trying her wings, reaching for some sort of independence that she hadn't had before. We were together here at the Mount a lot, and most of those times we were alone. Jane was a lovely, charming woman. The honest truth is that I could have responded to her, easily, even though she was a lot older than I was. But I didn't. That's the beginning and the end of the story.''

Susannah heard him out in silence. When he stopped, she stared at him, trying to see into his soul. She wanted to believe him.

"Do you really think I'm the kind of man who could make love to the mother, and then make love to the daughter? That I could do something like that and live with myself?''

At last, Susannah reached out to Paul, with both hands. She said, "No. I don't think you are that kind of person. But I had to be sure.''

She had been sure, when Paul was with her. When he held her for a while, kissed her softly, undemandingly, and then left. But later, when darkness and silence wrapped Laird's Mount like a shroud, she was no longer sure of anything.

# Chapter Eleven

As she drove down St. Andrews Road to keep her appointment with Barbara Blair, Susannah thought about the last and only time she'd been with the woman. It seemed aeons ago, yet it had actually been only three months.

*I'd been running,* thought Susannah with a kind of nostalgic longing. *But then the Judge died.* She hadn't run since.

She turned her car into the hilly driveway of the Blair House. On the way up, she sneaked a peek into the rearview mirror, remembering how she'd looked when she came here before—not great. She looked better today, with a touch of makeup and her hair smoothly combed, and a blue dress that complemented her gray eyes. Satisfied, Susannah parked and tucked the file folder, of her re-creation of Jane's research papers under her arm. She got out, closed the car door and automatically locked it. She'd been a city person for too long to be able to get used to the way Kinloch folks left their cars—not to mention their houses—unlocked all the time.

Barbara came out on the wide porch and waved a greeting. "Thought we'd sit out here—" she gestured to the rocking chairs "—since the weather's so pretty."

"That would be nice."

Settling into a rocker, Barbara remarked, "I got so used to seeing you running every morning, it's seemed strange to come out on the porch to get my newspaper and not see you down there. How've you been keeping yourself?"

"To myself, I guess." Susannah smiled ruefully. "I was thinking about that very thing as I drove up here today, that I don't run anymore. Of course, I get a different kind of physical exercise—I've been helping with the work at the Mount. But it's not the same. Maybe I should start running again."

"Why don't you do that? I know I said it was a fool thing to do, but that's just my big mouth. I said to Angelica Herbert in the bank the other day that it had been good to see such a healthy, strong young woman getting her exercise and I missed you. If you ask me, Angelica could use a little exercise herself—she's been looking a mite peaked."

"I'm sorry to hear that. I'll have to call her and invite her over one day soon. We've almost finished the restoration. In fact, even the rooms I've been living in are being painted their original color. But—" Susannah got down to business "—I didn't come to talk to you about that. Not exactly. The reason I'm here is that I've been trying to retrace the research my mother did on Laird's Mount before her death, and I thought perhaps you could help. I went to the library, but didn't find much.''

Barbara Blair linked her hands across her wide lap and rocked thoughtfully. ''That's because there's not much to find. Now, if the preservation society could afford to hire somebody to keep up with things, and if we had a place for an office... But you didn't come to talk about that, either, did you?''

The question was rhetorical. Susannah smiled, trying not to be impatient.

''Seems to me we talked about some of that when you were here before. What, precisely, is it that you think I can help you with?''

''I was hoping you'd save me some time—I know I can go to the county courthouse and look up transfers of deeds, but what I really want to know is the names of the people who have lived in Laird's Mount, and the years they were there.''

''Oh, that's no problem. I've got that right up here—'' she tapped her temple ''—in my head. You just hand me something to write with and I'll put it all down for you.''

This was exactly what Susannah had hoped for. She dug a pen out of her purse and handed it, along with a pad of paper from her file folder, to Barbara. ''While you're writing, I think I'll go around to the side of the house and take a look at your kitchen dependency. Do you mind?''

''No, not a bit. You go right ahead.''

Barbara's old kitchen building was much smaller than Susannah's, and filled with garden tools. It had a similar large fireplace and oven openings, but no trapdoor leading down to a root cellar. After a brief inspection, Susannah returned to the porch and resumed her seat in the rocker.

Barbara returned the pad, saying, "This is complete, except for one thing, but I expect that's not important. I told your mama the same."

"What's that?"

"For a few years after the last Richardson twin died, the estate officer at the bank was handling the property. You know, until the heirs could decide what they wanted to do with it. And for a while, they rented the house out. The bank handled it. I have no idea who the renters were. The only thing I know is that none of them lasted long, and they never settled down in Kinloch and became part of the community—if they had, I'd have known who they were. I expect the reason none of them stayed was the, you know—"

"The ghost?"

"That's it," said Barbara, leaning back and rocking vigorously. Her face took on its stern expression. "You seem like a mighty determined young woman. I expect you're just what that place needs. That's what I said to Adelaide—she's the president of the preservation society this year. I said, 'You mark my words, Addie, that young woman is going to stick it out!'"

"Thanks for the vote of confidence. I'm determined to do that. And thanks, too, for your time." Susannah half rose, then at Barbara Blair's next words, she sat down again.

"'Ghost or no ghost,' I said." She raised her faded brass eyebrows. "The ghost isn't bothering you none?"

"Not at all. I guess I'm just not sensitive to the spirit world. I've heard only some people can see them." The subject made her nervous, though. There was a defensive edge in her voice as she continued. "I've had some problems sleeping, but that's only because I haven't quite adjusted to all the changes in my life."

Barbara Blair clucked. "Poor child, to lose both your parents within a few months of each other. I'm sure it's been a shock, but you've been getting right on with your life and that's the important thing. Now," she added, a gleam appearing in her eye as she reached into the pocket of her ample denim skirt, "since all of us in the preservation society are in agreement that you're likely to become a permanent member of our community, and since you were so good as to put the historic covenants on the Mount, we want you to fill out this little membership card and give us a donation, and then you'll be a full-fledged member. As well you should be." She handed a slightly rumpled white card to Susannah.

"You're right," Susannah agreed—while she thought about there being no such thing as free advice. "I should join. I'll do it right now, and leave my check with you, if I may."

"You most certainly may," Barbara Blair chuckled, sounding pleased with herself and rocking up a storm.

SUSANNAH WAS MORE than halfway home from Barbara Blair's when she realized that she ought to find something else to do. She needed to stay out of the way of the painters. The dashboard clock said eleven-thirty, a little too early for lunch, though lunch with Angelica Herbert was a possibility.

As she cruised down the town's main street, Susannah wondered why she found it so impossible to like Angelica. She simply could not warm up to the woman. Briefly she considered adding Angelica's name to her mental list of people who might have had a reason to want Jane Hathaway dead. If Jane had been having an affair with Charles Herbert, that might be a motive. Angelica always seemed so stressed, that's why she was so hard to be around. Perhaps she was only that way with Susannah, perhaps she made her nervous because she had a guilty conscience about Jane

No, Susannah decided as she looped around the block. No to lunch, and no to Angelica as a suspect. If Jane had not died a natural death, if this whole thing wasn't some wild imagining on Susannah's part, then the person responsible had been cold, calculating and clever. Angelica was none of the above. Susannah's biggest problem was that those three characteristics did fit the Judge, at least when he was in his see-justice-done frame of mind, and they didn't fit anyone else Susannah knew in Kinloch.

On impulse, Susannah swung the car around and headed in the direction of Marvin Bradley's house and office. Perhaps he would be free to have lunch with her. Doctors had to eat, he was bound to take a lunch break around this time, and she was guaranteed a warm welcome. She had delayed asking Marvin the question she'd asked Paul and Charles. Not that Marvin was on her mental list; he'd been so concerned that his paperwork look right in case of an investigation into the Judge's suicide, he'd have had a heart attack himself at the very idea that he might be a suspect in any death. Marvin Bradley just didn't have enough nerve to murder anyone.

As she thought of murder, Susannah grimly realized how far she'd come. Was she half-insane herself to be thinking this way? Maybe, but she really couldn't help it, nor could she rest until she was sure she'd left no stone unturned. Anyway, she had to ask Marvin about his relationship with Jane, just to be thorough.

Once more there was no one at the reception desk when Susannah entered Marvin's Victorian house. She called out, "Hello? Marvin, are you here?"

"Susannah, is that you?" With a pink flush of pleasure on his cheeks, Marvin came quickly up the hall from the back of the house. "How nice to see you!" He took both her hands and stepped back, appraising her appearance. "I hope this unexpected visit doesn't mean that you are ill."

"No," she said, retracting her hands from his grip, "I'm fine. I'm just at loose ends and it's lunchtime, and I was hoping you were free."

"It's Saturday, my dear, in case you've forgotten. I only see emergencies on Saturdays and I'm free as a bird. I was just catching up on a little lab work. I do my own, so far as I can. And upstairs in my own little domain I have some marvelous chicken salad prepared by my housekeeper. Perhaps I can tempt you to eat here?''

Susannah would have preferred to go out, but there was no real reason to. She'd been alone in her own house with Marvin plenty of times, surely it would be no different being alone in his. "That would be very nice.''

"I'll just go put things away and wash my hands, and then we'll go up.''

Marvin's dining area was directly over his office, in the round turret. The chicken salad was indeed very good, and the view from the turret windows was pleasant. Her unexpected visit had had the desired effect on the doctor—he was practically falling all over himself to be congenial. Which made it hard for Susannah to broach the subject she intended to bring up. Finally, she did.

"Marvin, there's something I want to ask you, and I hope you won't take it the wrong way.''

He put his fingertips together in his listening pose, but he was smiling. "We'll just have to see, won't we?''

"I understand, from some things that various people around town have said to me, that you had a rather close relationship with my mother.''

He jumped at the question. "Jane Hathaway was my patient.''

"It has been implied that she may have been more than that to you, and I was hoping you'd tell me the truth. Were you having an affair with Jane?"

Marvin did not react in any of the ways Susannah might have expected. What he did was pout, rather prettily. "My, my, my, what a question. How am I supposed to answer that?"

"Honestly, I hope. Marvin, if you haven't figured it out already, my mother and I were not as close as most mothers and daughters. I won't hold it against you, I'd just like to know the truth."

His pale blue eyes glittered. "I can't tell you. Jane was my patient. Anything that happened between us was confidential."

Susannah did not like the way she was beginning to feel. Nevertheless, she pushed on. "But she's dead now, and I have a good reason for asking. Surely, since I'm her daughter and she's not here to be hurt by anything you reveal, you could tell me?"

Dr. Bradley moistened his shapely lips with his tongue. "Why do you want to know, Su-san-nah?" He drew out the syllables of her name teasingly. "Could the daughter be just a teeny bit jealous of the mother?"

Susannah's heart raced, and she felt sick to her stomach. She felt that Marvin Bradley had given her his answer, and she understood. She got to her feet in one swift motion that sent her purse, which had been on her lap, tumbling to the floor. She declared hotly, "Of course I'm not jealous of Jane! If you must know, I've been asking some other men in town the same thing. And the reason I'm asking, Dr. Bradley, is that I'm convinced that my mother did not die a natural death. And I don't think any ghost scared her to death, either! What I think is that somebody Jane made very uncomfortable killed her!''

With that declaration, Susannah scooped her purse up off the floor and stalked out of Marvin Bradley's house.

SHE OPENED HER EYES to utter blackness and wild, heart-pounding disorientation. For a few terrified moments she did not know where she was. She did not know if she was really awake, or if she was asleep and dreaming that she'd opened her eyes on this black void. As Susannah stared and tried to control the racing of her heart, the blackness before her eyes seemed to recede. And with it, the intensity of her terror.

Then she realized that she was in fact awake. She reached out her left hand and touched the newel post of the small stairway to the third floor of Laird's Mount. In the gloom of the high hall she could barely see it, and the stairs rose before her and then turned before they disappeared from view. Only this afternoon she'd removed the folding gate that had barred these stairs. One more step forward—a step that even now her feet wanted to take—and she would have begun to ascend. The darkness of the long-closed rooms above seemed to call her, to pull her upward. Susannah's right leg bent at the knee, her foot reached for the first stair.

Disoriented again, and confused, Susannah snatched her foot back. She looked down. Her feet were bare, and very white beneath the hem of her long nightgown. She turned her head and found the elongated rectangles of the two windows. Through their many small panes she saw a lighter shade of darkness, and she knew that the moon was still up although it did not shine directly through the windows. It was night. She had gone to bed. Ripples of anxiety spread beneath the surface of Susannah's skin as her mind tried to grasp a reality that her will wanted to deny: she had walked in her sleep! But why? She was not a sleepwalker, she'd never, ever done that before, so why?

And why even now, as she shivered and turned to make her way back to her room, did she want so much to climb those stairs?

# *Chapter Twelve*

Paul Starbuck felt heavy and slow and morose. He'd done something he almost never did—got drunk, at home, all by himself—and now he was paying for it. Served him right. Even Wolf wasn't interested in his company this morning.

After showering and shaving and forcing himself to eat some breakfast, he felt marginally better. He rummaged in the drawer of the small table near his front door until he found his sunglasses, put them on to guard his eyes against the bright sunlight that was bound to jar the remains of a whopper headache, went outside and sat down on the porch steps to think. It was Sunday. He didn't have to work today, but he wanted to. He wanted to see Susannah. Fat chance! Well, if he couldn't see her, he could think about her. In a more objective, less maudlin way than he'd been thinking about her last night when he drank all that beer. The memory made him wince. No sense feeling guilty, what was done was done.

He didn't know what to do. Things had been going great the other night . . . until they'd gone back to the

Mount. Then she'd changed, started pushing him away, asking all those questions about Jane. So he'd been honest—what else could he have said, what else could he have done? Susannah hadn't liked it but she'd believed him. Hadn't she? Paul rubbed his head again. He'd been all over this territory last night, and it wouldn't do any good to go over it again.

Wolf came bounding up with a red Frisbee in her mouth. She dropped it at Paul's feet, then looked at him expectantly.

"I thought we'd lost this," said Paul, picking it up. He asked without much enthusiasm, "You want to play?"

The big dog tossed her head and pawed excitedly.

Paul gave the red disk a halfhearted fling, and Wolf was off like a shot, racing the trajectory. With great strength and uncanny accuracy she launched herself into the air at just the right moment and snapped the Frisbee between her jaws. Paul grinned, and his heavy mood lightened a bit. He came down the steps and made a few more throws, trying not to think anymore. But it was no good—Susannah tugged at his mind and at his heart. He had to see her.

Paul curved his arm and let the disk fly high and wide. Wolf took off again, a black-and-silver blur, racing down almost to the river in pursuit. This gave him an idea—he would take Wolf for a walk. They'd walk along the riverbank as far as the Laird's Mount land, and then up to the house across the gently sloping fields. Before Susannah had moved in, Paul had often gone that way. As Wolf loped back to him, he

had a further inspiration—he'd ask Susannah to walk
back here with him and he'd make lunch for the two
of them. Yeah, it would be a good Sunday outing,
low-key, just the right touch.

When Wolf presented the Frisbee this time, Paul
took it and stowed it on the porch. The dog cocked her
head to one side and gave him a "what are you doing
that for?" look. Paul grinned and said, "Come on,
old girl, let's go for a walk. Let's go see Susannah!"

*Walk* was a word Wolf understood. She bobbed her
head up and down in agreement, barked, and was off,
prancing ahead of him.

Everything was greening up along the banks of the
Tuscarora, which was more stream than river down
here. The path would soon be overgrown if Paul didn't
do some cutting back. The last storm had blown a fair
number of dead branches off the trees at the water's
edge. They'd make good kindling, if they weren't bug
infested. He resolved to put some work in down here
soon, and then his thoughts turned once more to Susannah.

Paul wasn't needed at Laird's Mount anymore. All
his work was finished, except for the painting, and he
had painters who could do that better than he. He'd
done a good job—hell, he'd done a brilliant job and
he knew it—so why didn't he feel the satisfaction that
he usually felt when a job was finished? Because he
was worried about Susannah, that was why. Because
he'd feel better if he stuck around and helped her up
on the third floor. But she wanted to do it alone, and
he'd seen for himself that she was right, those rooms

were in such good shape that they didn't need much more than a good cleaning. He'd already had a glazier replace the broken windowpanes. There really wasn't anything else to do.

On the other hand, his North Carolina job really needed him. He'd stayed away for too long as it was, and he'd promised to go down on Tuesday and stay for the rest of the week. When he came back from there he'd have to check out other possible jobs that had come up. Life had to go on, and if Susannah wouldn't accept him in her life as…what? Lover? Friend? Both, Paul decided, he wanted to be both those things to her. If she wouldn't let him, then he would have to accept that he wouldn't be seeing much of her anymore.

Paul's heart lurched unhappily in his chest. He stuck his hands in his pockets and concentrated on Wolf, who was having a great time investigating nooks and crannies that only she could see among exposed tree roots. He wondered if he was destined to spend the rest of his life with only a female dog for a companion.

After walking a couple of miles along the riverbank, Paul reached the cleared lands of Laird's Mount. From here the first rise hid all but the roof and chimneys of the house from view. The roof alone was enough to make Paul nervous. There was something about Susannah being alone there that he didn't like. It was a kind of hunch, an instinct, a vague sense of something being not quite right. Lately he hadn't found anything out of place when he arrived in the mornings, but that hadn't eased his worry. As his crew had neared the end of the job, there hadn't been all that much to leave out. He still had this irrational feeling that someone or something was prowling around there at night.

Paul topped the first rise and the whole back side of the house came in sight. It was quite a place, all right. The bricks glowed the rich, deep red of old terra-cotta, a striking contrast to the blue of the sky and the green of lawns and trees. The back porches that he'd built on both sides of the main block were nicely symmetrical, their white trim clean and shining. The newly painted white shutters set off the red brick and enhanced the large windows in a way that was exactly right. Paul paused and drew in a long, appreciative breath. He felt pride in this work. But he was still concerned about Susannah.

He started walking again. In five or ten minutes he'd reach the house. Wolf had gone off on her own, but that was no problem, the dog knew this territory and would come if he called. Paul wondered if he should warn Susannah about the ghost at Laird's Mount. Maybe it was the ghost that made him anxious about her.

Paul had never actually seen the ghost at Laird's Mount. What he'd seen was a large, looming patch of shadow, at the base of the stairs to the third floor. Whether it moved around the house or not, he didn't know. He'd seen it more than once, always in that same spot, and he hadn't liked it so he'd just moved off and let the thing be. There was a bad, heavy kind of feeling to the thing that had made Paul think that something pretty terrible had happened in that person's life to make him—or her—hang around after death.

Wolf came tearing out of the trees at the edge of the lawn, long, rapid strides eating up the grass as she bounded clear across to the other side and disappeared again. Paul thought about the one time Wolf had been with him when he'd seen the shadowy patch that he thought was a ghost. If there was such a thing as a psychic dog, Wolf was it. She'd had no doubt that there was something on those stairs, and Paul would have been willing to bet his life that Wolf could see it much better than he could. She'd started to growl, and she'd seemed to grow in size because all her shaggy hair stood on end. Her eyes had narrowed and glowed like yellow fire. Never had his dog looked more feral, more dangerous than she had at that moment.

This gave Paul an idea. He wouldn't say anything to Susannah about the ghost, because if it wasn't bothering her he didn't want to put ideas in her head, but he would ask her to keep Wolf at the Mount for him while he went down to the North Carolina job. Wolf would protect Susannah from ghosts or anything else that might threaten her.

As he came up to the house, Paul saw a window open on the third floor. Susannah must be working up there. He cupped his hands around his mouth and yelled, "Hello up there! Anybody home?" No response. He yelled again.

Susannah leaned out of the window, her honey gold hair swinging forward. She looked pleased to see him, and Paul's heart did a flip. She called down, "Paul! You're just the person I want to see. Have you got your key or shall I come down and let you in?"

He fished in his pocket and brought out the Laird's Mount keys. He held them up, feeling a smile on his face so wide that his cheeks almost ached. "I got 'em. I'm coming up!"

He took the main stairs two at a time. For a moment he frowned at the large second-floor hall— they'd just gotten this place looking good, and now there was a big mess. But of course, Susannah had been throwing things down here as she cleaned out the rooms upstairs. He picked his way over a pile of magazines that looked old enough to belong in a museum, and around the broken slats of something that might once have been a baby's crib. For just a moment he hesitated at the bottom of the steps, but there was no sinister dark patch, only broad daylight streaming through the tall windows. Mustn't think about such things. He went on up the stairs, which were narrower and steeper than the main flight.

At the top there was a large landing, almost a room in itself, and off that to the right, a small room. The largest room was ahead, and there he found Susannah. She wore jeans cut off just above the knees—exquisite knees—and a faded plaid cotton shirt with the tail hanging out, and she looked great. Paul beamed and said, "Hi!"

"This is the most wonderful space!" Susannah declared, spinning around, arms out, a dust rag in one hand. "I had no idea it would be so large until I got most of the clutter out. I love it. Don't you?"

Paul looked around critically. "Yeah. I can see you've been working like a Trojan."

"Tom Parrish helped. He got here early and worked up until about half an hour ago, and then he left to go to church with Sarah. Paul, this is like finding an added bonus in a house that was already almost perfect. I'm going to use this room for my studio. I can already see how it will look, with my drafting table over there by the window to catch the light, and a long table and chairs for conferences with clients over there against that wall. And out here—" she breezed by him through the door to the sizable open area "—I'll have the business-type stuff, you know, a desk and telephone and all that, and I think I'll have shelves built along the side. The filing cabinets can go in the smaller room, I'll use it for storage space. Do you think we could put a half bath in part of the smaller room? I mean, I know it will fit, but can we get the plumbing up here?"

Her enthusiasm was catching. Paul immediately grasped Susannah's vision, and his mind started working with hers. He said, "Yeah, sure, we can come up between the ceiling below and this floor." He rubbed his chin thoughtfully, muttering, "The bath will have to be on this side of the room, we can put up an interior wall here..."

Susannah followed, listening, questioning, agreeing. When they'd figured out the half-bath idea, they returned to the large room. She had begun to clean the grime from the walls and woodwork. "I'm using plain soap and water. I didn't want to use harsh detergents on this two-hundred-year-old paint. Just look at this gorgeous color!"

Paul was looking. He wasn't familiar with the unusual color, even considering his experience with old homes, but then by the time he got to a house there were usually layers and layers of paint over whatever the original had been. This was a grayish blue-green, a little deeper than aqua but not as bright as turquoise. All the woodwork, including a wainscot halfway up all the four walls, was painted this interesting color. The upper half of the walls was aged to a buff color. "This is nice," he agreed, "very nice. I didn't realize the space had so much potential."

"And look at these lovely little doors," said Susannah, pointing to either side of the room where there were indeed two small doors set into the wainscoting. "What do you suppose they were for? They look like they're for children, but of course they couldn't go anywhere."

"Have you opened them?"

"No. That one's stuck, and the other one had stuff in front of it until just a couple of minutes before you came. To tell you the truth, I feel kind of reluctant, but I can't think why. Maybe you'll do it?"

"In a minute. Let me think." Paul studied the room, judging its measurements and comparing them to the blueprint of Laird's Mount that existed in his head. "There must be attic-type storage space beyond those little doors. The rooms on this floor were obviously meant to be lived in, but no one would have built a house without space for all the things people used to put in attics. Let's look and see if I'm right."

He was. Without a flashlight it was impossible to see much, but enough. Susannah stuck her head in and back out immediately. "Ugh! I don't want to go in that narrow space. Whatever's in there can just stay in there for another two hundred years."

"I don't know about that. If there are papers and other flammable things, you have a potential fire hazard. If you don't want to get in there yourself, have someone else do it."

"All right. I'll get to it eventually."

"Good. Now, if I can entice you to stop work for a while, I came by to suggest a walk by the river. Then over to my house, where I'll fix you something delicious for lunch. Good exercise followed by good food. An unbeatable combination."

"I don't know—" Susannah looked around at the room "—I'm kind of on a roll here."

"Omelets. I do great omelets, and you can choose your own filling. Bacon, cheese, ham, onions, mushrooms, broccoli, asparagus, fine herbs—"

Susannah laughed and tossed her dust rag into the air. "You talked me into it!"

PAUL MIGHT HAVE TALKED Susannah into lunch, but he couldn't talk her into anything else. She refused to look after Wolf while he was in North Carolina, pointing out that Paul had taken the dog with him on other such trips. He'd made up a tale that sounded plausible to him, about how Wolf kind of got in the way and the family he stayed with when he was down there didn't really like dogs, but Susannah wouldn't buy it. She said she liked Wolf well enough, but only when Paul was around. Alone with that big dog, she'd be nervous, and besides, Wolf would be in the way around her house, too. She intended to work hard on the third floor and didn't want any distractions. When Paul persisted, she was perceptive enough to declare that she suspected he didn't want her to look after his dog, but the other way around—and she didn't need anyone, man or beast, to look after her.

So Paul had to back down. He didn't give up, though. Late Sunday afternoon he drove over to Tom Parrish's house. By that time, Paul had persuaded himself that Susannah had been very foolish in her insistence that she didn't need an alarm system in her house, and she wouldn't even discuss it until the place was completely furnished. He had persuaded himself that someone, maybe just a drifter, but maybe someone more sinister, had been hanging around Laird's Mount at night. He had so completely convinced himself that he had no difficulty convincing Tom. Paul told Tom that he would pay him to act as night watchman and stay in the old kitchen dependency during the three nights that he would be away. He even took along his shotgun and gave it to Tom "just in case." Susannah was not to know. She was not to be alarmed.

Tom Parrish, who said he and Sarah were fond of Susannah and wouldn't let anything happen to her for anything in the world, agreed to become a watchman for Laird's Mount. And on the second night of his vigil, Tom Parrish died.

"IT WAS A HEART ATTACK," Susannah explained, tears welling in her eyes and spilling down her cheeks. It was odd how easily she cried for Tom, when with her own parents the tears had stayed locked up inside. "Sarah came up here looking for him, and she found him in the old kitchen, but he was dead. Oh, Paul, it was so awful for her! I had so many questions, but I couldn't ask her any of them. If you could only have seen the expression on her face, such grief and such dignity at the same time. So I have no idea why Tom Parrish was in that little building. He had a shotgun with him, but Sarah wouldn't take it home. She said leave it there, she didn't want it. But of course I couldn't leave it, I brought it in the house. I wish you'd take it away, I don't like having a gun in the house."

Paul had a look on his face that she'd never seen there before, that she couldn't read. She'd driven over to his house and left a note on the front door asking him to call the moment he returned, but he hadn't called, he'd just come. He passed a big hand over his face as if to rub all expression away and asked, "When did it happen?"

"Wednesday night, Sarah found him Thursday about noon. Yesterday. I wanted to call Marvin Bradley but Sarah wouldn't hear of it. She said Tom had a bad heart, and she asked to use the phone and called a funeral home. They came out with a hearse and took

Tom's body away. That may not have been the right way to handle it, but it was what Sarah wanted and I wasn't going to go against her. Not at a time like that.

"I'm glad you're back, Paul." Susannah twisted her hands together nervously. "I needed someone to talk to. I felt—I feel—anxious, I guess."

"I'm sure you do." Now Paul's face took on an expression that was easy to interpret but unnerving to see: a black, ominous scowl. "I don't like this, Susannah."

"It's creepy. Too many people are dying, due to natural causes or not. It seems to be happening all around me!"

Paul opened his arms, hesitantly, but Susannah did not hesitate. She went into them and let those strong, warm arms enfold her, allowed herself to feel secure. Blessedly safe, at least for a little while.

He stroked her hair and she felt the softness of his mouth at her temple. Slowly the tension drained from Susannah's body. Paul gripped her more tightly as he said, "I have to leave you for a while. I must go to see Sarah Parrish. But I'll be back."

Susannah moved out of his arms. "Take the shotgun to her, please. I really don't want it here. It's in the next room."

"No, Susannah. The shotgun didn't belong to Tom. It's mine. And Tom Parrish's death is on my head." He turned and strode away across the lateral hall so quickly that Susannah did not have time to get over her astonishment at what he'd said.

She stood looking at the door that closed behind him, doubts and questions crowding her mind. A tremor began in her shoulders and traveled through her whole body until her fingertips quivered. She needed somebody to trust, she couldn't handle everything alone anymore. But trusting was so risky! What had he meant? Could she trust Paul? Not love—no, that was too big a step, too much to hope for—but simple trust?

"This has got to stop," Susannah whispered to no one as she sank down on the edge of her bed.

# Chapter Thirteen

More than an hour passed, and still Paul did not return. Susannah grew tired of waiting for him, and more tired still of her own indecision. The furniture catalogs she'd been going through as a first step in furnishing the house did not hold her interest. She needed to work with her hands, and there was still some scrubbing to be done in the smaller room on the third floor. She changed into paint-spattered chinos and a blue work shirt, got her supplies and climbed the two flights of stairs. As she had since the night she'd awakened from sleepwalking, she felt pulled to the top floor. She had rationalized that this was because she had a deep need to get on with her professional life, and the top floor offered a space in which she could do it.

The need must have been very deep-seated, because since she had begun work up here the sleepwalking had stopped. But not the dreams; the dreams were something else again. Something that lingered, unfinished, between herself and her mother. She wouldn't think about the dreams now.

As Susannah worked the skies clouded over and the light, inside and out, took on a purplish hue. She didn't notice. She was completely absorbed in washing the overmantel above the fireplace. Stroking carefully with her wet cloth, Susannah appreciated the simple lines of the wood paneling. Less elaborate than the carved marble surrounds of the fireplaces in the rest of the house, but in its simplicity, just as beautiful.

Suddenly Susannah's cloth hit a snag along the right side of the overmantel. She looked and could see nothing, then felt with her fingers. If the wood were splintered or cracked, it would have to be repaired. There! Her fingertips found a loose spot where the wood had pulled away from the wall behind. She felt along it, frowning in the dim light as she tried to determine the extent of the crack.

The atmosphere in the small room darkened. Outside, a steady rain began to fall. The wind sounded like a huge sigh as it echoed through Laird's Mount. Preoccupied with her task, Susannah registered these changes only on the outer borders of her mind.

Her fingertips touched something that was neither the wood of the paneling, nor the plaster of the wall, but—"Paper!" Susannah exclaimed. A piece of paper was wedged behind the overmantel. It must have been deliberately hidden. Slowly, carefully, she worked the paper out of its hiding place. It was a sheet of heavy paper of good quality, only slightly yellowed with age, and had been folded in half. All of one side and part of the other were covered with slanted script in a style of penmanship that few people knew how to write anymore. Straining her eyes, Susannah now noticed how dark the room had become, and she heard the rain on the roof. There were no lights yet on the third floor, but she did not want to wait to read this interesting find. She sat down on the floor, squinted slightly, and began to read.

I, Daniel Richardson, have been kept a prisoner on the top floor of this house by my twin brother David for so long that I have lost count of time. He has boarded up the stairway and keeps a door at the bottom chained and locked from the outside. I used to pound on that door and yell at the top of my voice, but he no longer brings me enough food for strength, only enough to keep me barely alive. He hates me, he has always hated me. We are like two sides of a coin, only one side is dark and the other is light. David is the dark side, he is evil. I only hope that when I die—for I cannot live much longer—he will not go on to torture others the way he has tortured me. He told the world outside Laird's Mount that I died long ago. He had a funeral for me and buried an empty coffin in the family graveyard, and then came up here to my prison and told me all about it. Since then he has been slowly starving me to death. Once, I thought there was hope. I thought I had found a way out, but that proved to be false. I have no more hope. I have decided to help David. I will starve myself. The chamber pot can

have my water, the mice, my food. For them, it
will be a feast, for me, it is only a prolongation of
torture. I have but one prayer—that someday
someone will find this testament and know how
David Richardson murdered his twin brother
Daniel by means of slow starvation.

The paper was neither dated nor signed, but it didn't
need to be. Susannah whispered, "Oh God, how terrible!"

The wind that sounded like a sigh reverberated
again through Laird's Mount. The paper in Susannah's hand trembled like a blown leaf. A feeling that
she was no longer alone in the room made the tiny
hairs along her arms stand on end and she looked up,
toward the doorway. There she saw a shape, like a
shadow where there could be no shadow. Simultaneously she felt tremendous, overwhelming sorrow, so
heavy that her body could hardly bear it. Yet even as
she saw and felt it, the shadow dissolved and the heavy
weight of sorrow lifted. They were gone so quickly
that Susannah could not be sure that she had not
imagined the whole thing.

She looked at the paper in her hand, pressed it to her
breast. Sympathetic tears formed in the corners of her
eyes. No, she had not imagined any of this. She had
found the testament of Daniel Richardson—and in
finding it, she had set the ghost of Laird's Mount free.

BY THE TIME PAUL RETURNED, Susannah had show-
ered and dressed in her favorite lavender sweat suit for

warmth as the chilly rain continued to fall. She had
made a pot of vegetable soup from scratch, set it to
simmer on the new stove in her new kitchen, and now
its delicious fragrance filled the downstairs rooms.
Thinking that Paul would be hungry, she prepared to
feed him for once, instead of the other way around.
She was setting the table and singing along with a
classic rock station on her portable radio when she
heard him knock at the front door.

She opened the door and greeted him with a daz-
zling smile. "You're back! Come in, I have the most
amazing thing to tell you. And show you."

Looking puzzled by the transformation in Susannah, Paul let her lead him by the hand into her room.
She seated him in the recliner, pulled over one of the
ladder-back chairs for herself, then handed him a piece
of paper. "Read it," she said, her eyes dancing.

Paul did, and when he had finished, Susannah told
him the rest, where she'd found it, what she'd seen and
felt. She concluded, "The ghost that so many people
said was in this house was the ghost of Daniel Richardson. He was waiting around for someone to find
this testament, he wanted the world to know. I found
it, so he's satisfied. And now he's gone."

"You're right," said Paul, "it's amazing. I didn't
know that you were aware of the ghost, Susannah. I
wondered if I should tell you—"

"You mean you knew?"

"Yes, I did. I felt its presence—it was an oppres-
sive, heavy sort of feeling. One day I had Wolf with
me and she saw it, too. She liked it even less than I did.

I can't help but think maybe I should have told you about it."

"It doesn't matter now," said Susannah, pulling one foot up in the chair and hugging her knee to her chest, "because everything is going to be different now that it's gone. I don't think Daniel's ghost would really have harmed anyone intentionally, but after he left I could tell a difference, and now it all makes sense to me. I think his terrible sorrow filled this house. Especially at night. I did have trouble sleeping and I even caught myself walking in my sleep. And you know where I was? This is interesting, Paul. When I woke up I was standing right at the base of the third-floor stairs. Where he said his brother had put up a door. Daniel must have come down those stairs God knows how many times, trying to get out, and always had to stop in that very spot."

"That's where I encountered the ghost, too. And where it was when Wolf saw it more clearly than I ever did."

"After that night when I woke up there, I felt pulled to go up to the third floor. I think the ghost was somehow able to influence me, to keep me working up there until I found what he wanted me to find. Now that I've found it and he's gone, the house feels better, lighter. All that sadness is gone. Come on, we'll walk around. I'll bet you can feel the difference yourself."

They toured through all the rooms of Laird's Mount. Susannah was happy, really happy for the first time in so long that she could not remember. That is, not counting the night she'd danced with Paul—she'd been happy then, too, but the happiness had disappeared when they returned here. She was tempted to tell Paul that, and glanced at his face in profile, loving the way his hair curled around his ears and in the back. But no, she couldn't tell him. There was something else she could tell him, though—maybe even more important. As they descended once more to the first floor, she did.

"Paul, I have a recurring dream that I think will be banished forever by this walk we've just taken through all the rooms. In the dream I'm walking through Laird's Mount, but it's a nightmare, the rooms go on and on and on and there's something awful in the house. My mother is in the dream, too, somewhere ahead of me, luring me on. I've felt so happy just now, walking through my house with you. Surely the happiness is strong enough to make the dream go away, just as the ghost is gone."

Susannah stopped at the door to her room and took both Paul's hands in hers. Solemnly she said, "My mother can be at peace, too. I don't need to think anymore that someone killed her. There was no murder. Marvin Bradley was right. Mother saw the ghost and was so frightened that her heart stopped. That's the truth. That's my answer."

"Hmm," said Paul.

Later, after they'd both had bowls of vegetable soup and grilled cheese sandwiches, they lingered over coffee at the table. Paul pushed back his chair and crossed his ankle over the opposite knee. He cleared his throat, then said, "Susannah, I hate to rain on your parade, but I'm still feeling bad about Tom Parrish."

"Oh, of course. How is Sarah?"

"She's doing pretty well. All their children are gathering around her. They'll help."

Susannah looked at the shotgun propped in the corner, then back at Paul, noting his somber expression. "You said the gun is yours. What was Tom doing with it? And why did you say his death was on your head?"

His dark blue eyes studied her. "You were right when you accused me of wanting Wolf to look after you while I was gone. I did. I wanted you to have her in the house for protection. When you refused, I went over and told Tom and Sarah my concerns. I hired Tom to patrol the grounds and keep an eye on the house in my absence, told him he could stay in the old kitchen, and gave him my gun in case he needed it."

Susannah's initial reaction was anger. Her chin went up, her eyes flashed. "You had no right, no reason to do such a thing, Paul Starbuck!"

As always when Susannah flared up, Paul's own temper flared in response. He clenched his jaw, a vein at his temple pulsed visibly. "I was concerned about you, goddamn it! If you weren't as stubborn as an old mule, if you'd let me get an alarm in here the way I wanted to—"

"Are you trying to tell me that if I'd let you have the alarm installed, Tom Parrish would be alive today?"

"No! Of course not!"

"Yes, you are, you're trying to shift the blame off yourself and onto me." Susannah heard how her own words sounded and immediately was aghast. "Listen to us, squabbling like children, when poor Tom is dead. We should be ashamed of ourselves."

"Yeah. I'm sorry. Unfortunately, nothing is going to bring Tom back. Let me try again. What I wanted to say, Susannah, is that as glad as I am about the ghost being gone and all, I'm still worried about your safety."

"Why?" Susannah was genuinely puzzled.

"Because for some time I've thought someone was prowling around your house and grounds at night. I can't explain it exactly, it's just a kind of hunch. A very strong conviction that I can't prove."

"Well, you're wrong." She'd sounded more harsh than she meant to, so she leaned over and put her hand on Paul's ankle. "You have to understand, Paul, that I've always been very independent, ever since I was a child. Sometimes I've thought it would be nice to be looked after, but there was never anyone to do it, so I have no experience of that. Anyway, let's think about this conviction of yours from another point of view. I admitted that I've had trouble sleeping. I've been awake at various hours of the night, and I've never seen or heard any signs of an intruder."

He studied her some more. "It's a little too much of a coincidence to me that I should hire Tom to be night watchman and within two days he turns up dead. In exactly the same way your mother turned up dead, of a cardiac problem. You yourself, not long ago, said too many people were dying. I think it's damn suspicious, and I don't think you should be staying here alone until we get to the bottom of this!''

Susannah folded her arms across her chest. "You are one stubborn son of a you-know-what, Paul Starbuck."

"No more than you, Susannah Hathaway." Suddenly Paul smiled. "If we could ever get our stubbornness together, going in the same direction, we'd make a helluva team!"

Relenting, seeing his point, Susannah smiled back. Still, they had to deal with the things he'd brought up. She gathered her mental forces and began to do so. "I think what has happened here is that you've caught my paranoia. I never should have said that about too many people dying, so try to forget it, okay? Point number one, Mother did die a natural death, I'm sure of it now. Point number two, there was never any question about the Judge—he committed suicide, we know from the autopsy report that the drugs were found in his digestive system. Point number three, Sarah said that Tom had heart trouble, and he was not a young man. It's just very unfortunate that he had his fatal heart attack here, but really, Paul, it could have happened anywhere at any time."

Grudgingly Paul conceded, "You could be right."

"I'm sure I am. As for my paranoia, I think the ghost in this house had something to do with it. Charles Herbert said, and Barbara Blair implied, that Laird's Mount had not been a pleasant place for people to live. There was a kind of depressed aura about the house—it wasn't so obvious to me until it lifted this afternoon.''

"Oh, Susannah, I give up. You've overwhelmed me with your impeccable logic. Come here and let me hold you."

She did. And of course he did more than hold her. When at last he left, Susannah fell into bed and slept a long, delicious sleep. She dreamed that she was married to Paul. It was a wonderful, wonderful dream.

IT SEEMED THAT WITH the departure of the ghost, new life poured into Laird's Mount. Susannah had never been more busy. The buyer who'd been interested in her father's house finally came up to an acceptable price. The timing could not have been better—the Mount was ready to receive the furniture that she'd decided to keep. She hired movers and oversaw the transfer. Compared to all the things the Judge and Jane had crammed into their house, Susannah hadn't kept much, but it was enough to give her a taste of how glorious her own house would look when it was fully furnished.

Thus inspired, and armed with ideas culled from the catalogs she'd pored over, Susannah went on an orgy of furniture buying. The room she'd lived in for so long became a library, with the aid of handsome, glass-fronted mahogany bookcases that were not antiques but good reproductions whose scale was appropriate for a room much higher and bigger than most modern rooms. The music room became a formal parlor, its color scheme dictated by its yellow walls and Jane's Chinese rug, whose ivory background and predominantly amber floral border both fit and harmonized. Later Susannah intended to get a harpsichord for one corner, in homage to the room's original purpose. She left the corresponding room on the other side empty for the moment. It would eventually be a formal dining room and she would furnish it entirely with antiques that she intended to purchase at a leisurely pace. For now, she could eat at the refectory table that she had moved from her former one-room setup into the new kitchen.

Upstairs, she claimed the largest bedroom for her own. She divided it into sleeping and sitting areas. She found the bed of her dreams, a queen-size cherrywood reproduction with pencil posts. Without batting an eyelash she purchased a huge Oriental rug for her bedroom floor, its once predominant-red color faded to a lovely rose. Soft, cushy chairs were covered in a velvety fabric that picked up a secondary blue color from the rug; long ivory curtains had a tieback with a stripe of the same blue. The guest room, like the dining room, she left bare for now.

While Susannah was buying and installing furniture, a crew handpicked by Paul was constructing the half bath on the third floor. She ordered her drafting table and office furniture and equipment by catalog because she knew exactly what she wanted. It was delivered on the same day that the plumbers put the finishing touches on the bath.

Everything was coming together so beautifully. Susannah felt as if, at long last, the heavens were smiling on her. Except for one thing: she was still having the dream.

She didn't tell Paul. The dream didn't come every night, and she was so used to it by now that she would awaken, shrug it off, and go right back to sleep. She was looking more like her old self, gaining back the weight she'd lost in spite of chasing all over the Virginia countryside after furniture and dishes and curtains and towels and sheets and everything else.

Susannah's life settled into a routine that worked for her. Early every morning she would go for a run. Her own long driveway, smoothed and newly laid with fine-textured gravel under the watchful eye of the landscape architect, was a good surface to run on. About the time she finished her run the landscape architect and his workers would arrive, she'd consult with them, then go in and begin her own day. Her work at first was getting the house furnished, but with the arrival of the materials and equipment to set up her office and studio, she could take steps to resume her profession. Then she could have regular work hours, as she was accustomed to. Most evenings Paul walked over, accompanied by Wolf, to see what progress she had made that day. Sometimes she walked back with him to his house and ate a dinner that he prepared. Other times he stayed at the Mount and she cooked. She was growing more and more comfortable with him.

The night came, as she had known it would, when Paul did not go home. He stayed, and in the queen-size bed that was long enough to accommodate four very long legs, he made love to her. He was gentle and patient. He whispered and asked and coaxed, his fingers and lips and tongue finding all the right places, the secret places, until Susannah caught fire. She had never, ever, felt the way Paul made her feel—cherished, wanton, ecstatic.

When in the velvet darkness they lay blissfully exhausted in each other's arms and Paul said from deep in his throat, "I love you, Susannah," she heard herself reply, "And I love you, Paul Starbuck." It slipped out of her, that hardest of all things to say, as easily and smoothly as if she had been practicing the words all her life. Then, smiling and closing her eyes, she realized that she had been; she just hadn't had the right person to say them to aloud, until now.

Everything was perfect, absolutely perfect, until in the dead of night Wolf started to howl.

# Chapter Fourteen

"It's always something!" said Paul, looking at his own tired face in the mirror. Now Susannah was sleeping fine, and he wasn't—which was so unusual for him that it put him totally out of sorts.

He addressed Wolf, who was sitting at his feet while Paul shaved. "I sure wish you could tell me what you were doing out there in that old kitchen last week, howling your head off in the middle of the night."

Wolf panted and whined a little, softly, as if she too wished that she could tell him.

Paul turned back to his shaving and dismissed the dog. "Go on and eat your breakfast. I've got a lot of thinking to do." She stood up, waited a minute and watched to be sure she'd understood, and then padded away.

He wished he could stop thinking about that night, but he couldn't—probably because it had also been the first time he'd made love to Susannah. That part had been wonderful, and they'd even topped it a couple of times since then. It was just damn unfortunate that for him the good memory had been almost blotted out by the bad. For Susannah's sake Paul had tried to make light of Wolf's strange behavior the night they'd first made love, but he'd known that the dog wouldn't howl like that without a damn good reason.

He went back over it in his head for what seemed like the thousandth time. He'd woken from a deep sleep to hear the dog howling. He'd jumped right up and pulled on his trousers, asked Susannah where his shotgun was—thank goodness he'd never taken it back home—and retrieved it. By then, Susannah, who was determined to go with him no matter what he said, had joined him and they'd gone outside into a moonless night.

They'd stood there in the pitch-black dark, with their senses heightened to an excruciating level as they tried to figure out where Wolf's howling was coming from. Paul had tried to feel reassured by the fact that his dog was howling rather than growling and barking, because those were the things she did if she'd cornered a person or an animal that she considered a threat. But the howling was so eerie . . . Susannah had asked, rather shakily, if he was sure his "dog" wasn't one-hundred-percent wolf. He'd had to agree that Wolf sounded like a real wolf howling in the night.

Every time Paul went over this, he tried to see more detail in his memory, as if his mind might have recorded something that his eyes couldn't see in the dark. He tried to hear the same way. But he couldn't. It had been as if the darkness was so dense and heavy that it obscured everything in the universe. Everything except that awful howling.

He pondered over how long he and Susannah might have stood there before at last he got a bearing in the direction of the old kitchen. Long enough for whatever, whoever, had disturbed the dog to hide, or to get clean away?

Paul had crossed the lawn as fast as he'd dared to, the shotgun in one hand and Susannah's clutching grip in the other. The door of the kitchen dependency was open, an even blacker rectangle in the black night. And inside sat Wolf, her yellow eyes glowing as if from an inner source—there was no outside light. Of course, the dog's eyes were more sensitive than a human's and she'd been able to see much better than Paul and Susannah could. She'd stopped her eerie noise as soon as they appeared in the open door.

The really weird thing was that the dog wasn't trapped, and she hadn't cornered anything, either. All she was doing was sitting right in the middle of the floor. Right on top of the trapdoor. Though he hadn't said anything about it, that had seemed very, very strange. If only he'd thought to grab a flashlight—he'd cursed himself about that each of the thousand times he'd been over this.

Paul rinsed off his razor and then wiped his face. He tried to brush the curls out of his hair. That night, after he'd pursuaded Susannah to take the dog outside, he'd shut the door after them. Then he'd raised the trapdoor even though he knew he wouldn't be able to see a damn thing down there. He'd said viciously, "Come on out, I've got a shotgun trained on you!" He'd been plenty mad by then. A couple of seconds later he'd felt like a damn fool. Of course there hadn't been anybody down there.

The trouble was that there *could* have been somebody down there, if it was somebody with a hell of a lot of nerve. Somebody smart enough to know that he couldn't see them, and if they stayed quiet enough he couldn't hear them. Somebody quick enough to have scrambled out and run off in the five or so minutes that it had taken Paul to herd Susannah and Wolf back into the house and return with a flashlight. The inside of the root cellar had looked exactly the same as when he'd seen it before. Paul was ninety-nine percent certain that the ladder was right where it had been before, too. Probably he was continuing to worry and worry over nothing.

Paul went into his kitchen and poured himself a cup of the coffee that had brewed while he shaved. As he sipped, he tried to achieve a more positive frame of mind. Something good had come of that mysterious, unsettling episode—Susannah had at last agreed to have the alarms installed. She'd also promised to close and lock the gate—which had been repaired a good couple of months ago—every night. If anybody came through that gate or a door or a window, the alarm would not only sound, it would automatically dial two telephone numbers: first the police, then Paul Starbuck.

Of course, no alarm system would work unless it was turned on. This one wouldn't work unless everything—doors, windows, gate—was closed. And Susannah, as Paul now knew, liked to sleep with a window open.

And now, as if all that weren't enough to worry about, Susannah had gone and sprained her ankle! Running, she said. On her own driveway, she said. Tripped over nothing, accidents happen, she said.

"You know what?" Paul asked Wolf, who sat near the table looking at him expectantly. Wolf cocked her head and waited. "I'd like nothing more than to move in with Susannah. I'd keep her safe."

Wolf got up, padded over and put her head in Paul's lap. He scratched behind her ears idly. "We'd be great for her. If I were with her all the time I'd have driven her to Danville to get that ankle looked after. I wouldn't have let that creep Marvin Bradley put his hands on her ankle—or anywhere else!—for anything."

But Susannah had sprained her ankle on her morning run two days ago, and he hadn't found out until that evening. She'd called a cab to take her to Bradley's office and he'd taped it up and everything. He was probably a competent doctor even if he was a creep. She wouldn't be able to drive for a couple of weeks because it was the right ankle and she couldn't put any pressure on it, but she could get around the house okay. Or so she said. She didn't need any help. She didn't want Paul staying over until the ankle was better.

So Paul was leaving her alone. He was trying hard to understand this independent, spirited, determined woman he loved. He was trying to give her space, and time. "But, oh God, Wolf, I want her to marry me. Now!"

SUSANNAH LIMPED up the stairs to her studio space on the third floor. Climbing stairs took her forever—this sprained ankle was a pain in more ways than one! When she finally made it, she sat in the desk chair to rest for a minute. This landing area made a good office space, but the desk looked awfully bare. She thought about getting a computer. At the very least she should get a telephone up here. She must remember to call the telephone company when she went back downstairs.

Her ankle throbbed. She propped her foot on the desk. Susannah let her thoughts move to the Grand Plan that had been forming in her mind for the last several days. The Grand Plan now had a real name, at least in her head. Hathaway and Starbuck, Restorations.

A smile slowly spread over Susannah's face. Hathaway and Starbuck. It had a nice ring to it: Hathaway and Starbuck, Restorations! Being in love made her giddy, she only hoped it didn't cloud her judgment.

A business partnership with Paul was a good idea, maybe even a great idea. Of course, he already had a viable business, but he wasn't making big bucks. The big money, as Susannah well knew, was in large-scale projects, not single houses, no matter how grand. Adaptive uses that preserved the architectural integrity of a property, or a whole neighborhood of properties, turning them into offices, hotels, small businesses of various kinds—those were the things Susannah could do. She could also do complex structural analyses, the kind of thing Paul had to call an engineer in for to do Laird's Mount.

There was only one flaw in her plan. Well, maybe two. Paul really didn't seem all that interested in making big bucks. The money wasn't important to Susannah, either, at least not anymore, but the scale was. She liked the idea of preserving whole blocks of old buildings, and mansions that were so huge no one family would ever want to live in them, an historic old downtown . . .

The other flaw in her scheme was that even though Susannah thought they'd ended up working well together on Laird's Mount, Paul might not think so. He might just have been being polite and considerate of her feelings. As soon as she mentioned the idea of a business partnership, the old chip might come right back on his shoulder.

Susannah gingerly put her foot to the floor and got out of the chair, letting her good leg take her weight. The ankle bothered her more than she liked to admit. She half hopped, half limped into the large room that was her studio. The room was filled with lovely morning light. She made her way to the windows and opened both of them, letting in a soft breeze that brought with it the heady scents of late spring. The air was so clean and clear, the atmosphere so heavenly quiet. The only sound she could hear, if she listened hard enough, was the chirp and trill of birdsong. The rolling green lawns, the trees, the cloud-fluffed blue sky . . . to live and work in such surroundings was almost too much. She felt almost guilty having it all to herself. Susannah stretched, breathed deeply and felt another smile on her face.

Enough of that—time to get to work. Susannah sat at her drafting table, pulling a second stool over to prop her injured ankle on. She opened her large sketchbook. She had a possible project in mind, something Charles Herbert had put her on to, and she'd started some preliminary sketches. For now she was keeping this a secret from Paul; he was too deep in evaluating his own possible jobs, off looking at a different one every day. But at the right time, when she was ready and he seemed receptive, she'd tell him about the Grand Plan....

Susannah began to sketch. As happened when she was doing her best work, she completely lost track of time. She entered a kind of altered state in which she was aware only of the paper before her and the movements of the soft black pencil on the paper....

Her throbbing ankle brought her back into the room. She flexed her knee, put down her pencil and rubbed at the injury, though she knew that would do no good. The only thing that would help was another couple of aspirin—she balanced this knowledge against the thought of the trip downstairs, and decided against it. Then, with a critical eye she looked at her drawings...and gasped.

Susannah turned back page after page of her sketchbook. She felt oddly breathless, her mind could not grasp what she had done. She'd abandoned the architectural drawings many pages back, though she had no memory of doing so. On one page after another, over and over, she'd drawn a face. A face she had never seen before!

She had always been good at any kind of drawing, always excelled at capturing a likeness. The first sketches of the face were incomplete, as if she saw the model through a curtain, or a veil. She turned pages. They got better, clearer. She had drawn the face of a boy. An adolescent boy. He had that innocent, unformed look of maleness just emerging.

The very last sketch gave Susannah goose bumps. She had achieved a clarity that was almost photographic. And now, the boy seemed vaguely familiar. How had she done this? And why?

WOLF WAS CURLED UP in the middle of the braided rug on Paul's living room floor. She usually napped a lot while her master was gone in the daytime. Her ears twitched, and her tail; muscular ripples moved through her body. Her yellow eyes opened. Her head came up. She was very still, an intense expression on her wolfish face.

Paul's house was utterly silent, undisturbed. Wolf lifted her nose in the air, nostrils distended. She got up, front legs first, then hind legs. Her nails clicked when she left the rug and went to the window. She put front paws on the sill and stood on her hind legs, looking out. There was no one outside, but still Wolf gazed, intense, vigilant.

ABOUT THREE MILES outside of South Boston, Virginia, Paul Starbuck was tramping through a wreck of an antebellum mansion, trying to decide if it was worth working on or not. He'd asked the owner, a chatty woman whose presence was distracting, to leave him there on his own. Finally, after wasting a lot of his time, she'd left. Now he was going to be hard-pressed to finish his assessment while there was enough light to do it.

At the top of the stairs Paul wiped his brow. He had begun to sweat, though it wasn't particularly warm in here. In fact, it was cool in the dank, musty way of old houses that have been shut up for a long time. No, he didn't like this place one bit. He plodded on down the debris-strewn hall, thinking, *The sooner I get on with it, the sooner I can leave.*

WOLF BEGAN TO PACE back and forth, back and forth, along the length of Paul's living room. About every fourth transit, she would go to the window and look out. Her mouth was open, she panted. There was an anxious expression in her yellow eyes.

SUSANNAH STUDIED her drawings. She went back to the architectural sketch that she'd seemingly abandoned in midmotion. On the bottom of that page was the first face, rather small, little more than an outline. She turned to the next, and the next, fascinated by the way the features slowly emerged.

Suddenly alert, she raised her head and looked around the room. For the briefest second, she had a feeling that she could almost see the boy, there in the far corner. She rubbed her forehead, leaving a gray smudge from the pencil lead that had come off on her fingers.

Slowly she began to get an idea. Not that she had seen or drawn a ghost. This was different. She flipped

through the pages to the final one, the one that was
almost a photographic likeness. Surely at one time this
boy had been in this room!

HE WAS STANDING in front of a closed-up fireplace
whose mantel had been ripped away, when it hit him.
Paul blinked. He staggered back, confused, his sight
going suddenly dark. And then his whole mind filled
with two words: *Laird's Mount!*

"Susannah," he said, then more loudly, "Susannah!"

In that instant his sight cleared. The reason for all
the bad feelings about being in this house outside
South Boston also became clear. He had to leave, he
had to get back to Laird's Mount, because Susannah
needed him.

SUSANNAH HEARD A NOISE. A scratching, scrabbling
noise that seemed to come from the outside wall, behind the wainscoting. Mice, she thought. But no, mice
wouldn't make that loud a noise, and besides, she'd
had the exterminator out not long ago. Squirrels,
maybe, in the space under the eaves. What a bother!
Maybe, if she ignored them, they'd find their way out.

Now there was a heavy, solid sound. No squirrel had
made that. It had come from behind the little door in
the wainscoting. Strange...she didn't like this. But
then, for some reason she'd never liked those little
doors, anyway.

PAUL POUNDED DOWN the staircase, not looking where
he was going, and almost fell when a riser gave way.

He grabbed the handrail and kept himself upright, wrenched the hell out of his arm, but he didn't care. He jumped the bottom three steps and left the crumbling house at a dead run, pulling keys out of his pocket on the way. His feet skidded on the gravel drive as he barreled toward his truck and flung open the door.

He tore out of that driveway like a bat out of hell.

WOLF WHINED. She pawed at the front door, then scratched, her nails leaving long marks like claws. She whined louder, backed away from the door. She paced rapidly, head down, mouth open, showing her teeth, tongue hanging out. She began to back away from the window, her eyes taking on a feral gleam.

Backed up against the far wall of Paul's living room, Wolf threw up her head and gave one long, blood-curdling howl. The air in the room seemed to snap and crackle as the great dog gathered her energy. Her black-and-silver coat stood out around her body. Her muscles bunched, tensed. And then she ran, strong, loping strides that ended in a mighty leap. Glass shattered as Wolf hurled herself through the window.

SUSANNAH STARED in slowly growing horror as the little door in the wainscoting opened by itself.

# Chapter Fifteen

Fingers appeared, gripping the little door from the inside. Susannah was frozen in place on her stool at the drafting table. Then shoulders, as the door opened wider, and the top of a head.

"Well, well, well. Look who's here!" he said, raising his head and straightening up. Neatly he closed the little door behind him.

Her insides had turned to ice. All of a sudden her mind felt extraordinarily sharp, and her voice when she spoke had a cutting edge like a knife. "What the hell are you doing here, Marvin?"

He brushed off the shoulders of his white shirt, felt the knot in his tie, and inquired in a friendly voice, "How is your ankle, Susannah?"

She was not afraid. Not really, not yet. She said, "Come off it, Marvin! This is no house call. How did you get back there, and how long have you been there?"

"Oh, that's my little secret. I've been in and out this way many times, many times." He strolled around the room with his hands in his pockets, nodding appreciatively. "I must say, you've done a splendid job with Laird's Mount. This room in particular has never looked better, I daresay, since the house was first built. I couldn't have done better myself—that's why I decided to let you finish."

"*Let* me finish?" Susannah felt a stinging sensation behind her right ear. Automatically her hand went up to rub the spot.

"Oh, yes. Yes." He came within a few inches of where she sat, and reached out his soft, white, so-often-washed doctor's fingers. Susannah did not allow herself to flinch as he touched her. He said, "Tsk, tsk, you have a smudge on your lovely forehead. I'll just smooth it away—there. And now, allow me to help you down from that stool, my dear. Why don't we sit at that very nice table—a conference table, isn't it—and have a little chat."

Reluctantly Susannah gave him her hand. She didn't have much choice, and she didn't know whether to be afraid or not. There was something wrong with him, that much she could see. His slightly protuberant eyes had a look that was not normal. His eyes...

"Wait a minute, Marvin." Susannah turned back to the drafting table and picked up her sketchbook. "There's something I want to show you."

"Bring it to the table then, Susannah. I'm sure with your bad ankle you'll be more comfortable sitting down." He sat himself at the end of the table. Light from the window behind him mercilessly showed up the sparseness of his short, pale hair.

Susannah limped over and sat at midtable, with one chair between them. She flipped through the sketches

she'd made and chose one several pages back, when
the face was just becoming clear. She held the book up
in both hands and turned it to him. "That's you, isn't
it? When you were a boy."

Marvin frowned, as if he did not care for this dis-
traction. He did not reply.

Susannah slowly turned page after page, and on
each one the likeness grew sharper. "Look at the pictures, Marvin, and tell me, this *is* you, isn't it?"

The sketches had his attention now. Marvin narrowed his eyes. "I suppose it could be. As a boy. That
was a long time ago. Where did you get these drawings, Susannah?"

She turned the book around so that he could no
longer see. Yes, the final and best likeness was on the
next page. She turned it over, looked at what she'd
drawn and compared that face to the forty-something
face of the man at the end of the table. Yes, the set of
the head on the neck was the same, the narrow bone
structure, and the mouth had the beginnings of its
sensual shape. The eyes—they were the same and yet
not the same. In the boy's eyes she'd captured a
haunted, yearning expression that was very different
from the cold, probing eyes of the adult Marvin
Bradley.

"Let me see!" he demanded, an edge of hysteria in
his voice.

Taking her time, Susannah placed the sketchbook
flat on the table and pushed it toward him. "I did
these drawings myself, today. I was in a kind of a
trance, or something, when I did them."

Marvin's complexion, normally pale, was now completely drained of color. The shapely mouth gaped open as he gazed at the picture. He touched it with the fingers of one hand. "That's impossible," he gasped. "But it's me. It really is me!"

*He's gone crazy. I'm alone in my house with a madman. I've got to get him to tell me how he got in, and then somehow I've got to get him out of here.*

"Tell me *exactly* how you drew this picture. I have to know, right now!"

Susannah tossed her head, trying to keep up her usual spirits. "You wouldn't believe me."

He yelled, "Tell me!"

Susannah leaned back and propped her swollen ankle up on the empty chair between herself and the doctor who'd wrapped its elastic bandages. "Okay, I'll make you a deal, Marvin. I'll tell you how I did the drawings, if you tell me how you got in the house and behind that little door. Deal?"

"Deal," he said, adding nastily, "I was going to tell you anyway, so you haven't gained much. You needn't think you're so clever."

"I think I'm pretty clever. For instance, I know that when you were about, what—fourteen years old?—you were in this room. This very room. In fact, I'll bet you spent a lot of time in here because I *saw* you, Marvin. That's how I was able to draw you. Strange as it sounds, you left an impression of yourself here, and I picked up on it. Okay, that's my story. Your turn."

"You're dangerous, Susannah Hathaway," said Marvin, his pale eyes glittering. He had recovered his composure. "But not too dangerous for me." He leaned back, seemingly relaxed, and stuck his hands in his pockets.

The spot behind Susannah's right ear stung. Again. She ignored it, as difficult as that was to do. She didn't want to give this man any advantage, she couldn't let anything distract her, not even a bug or a spider on her neck, no matter how much she hated them. She wouldn't look very dangerous slapping at her hair, and if he wanted to think she was dangerous, that was fine with her. She raised her chin. "Well, as I said, it's your turn."

"In a minute. You surprised me with these pictures, but we're going to do this my way."

"Do what?" The fear she'd felt when the little door had opened tried to come back, but she pushed it away.

He ignored her question. "It's too bad you had to take up with that ill-mannered giant, Starbuck. There was a time there when I actually thought I could let you live."

Fear settled like a lump in Susannah's chest, and this time she could not push it away.

Marvin put his fingertips together and pulled them apart repeatedly. "Yes, I thought I might marry you and we could live here, the two of us, at least for a while. I'm not incapable of sex, you know."

"I never doubted that."

"How very gratifying! Now, to show you what a generous man I can be, I will satisfy your curiosity before we get on with our business of the afternoon. I believe we will continue to be quite alone here. I know that your friend, Mr. Starbuck, is out of town today. I've watched your house, Susannah, from my own private entrance, so to speak, and I know that you do not often receive unexpected company."

Susannah had to use every ounce of willpower to sit still in her chair, but she did it, and kept silent.

"You have discovered, no doubt, how thick these brick walls are? But neither you nor your restoration expert Mr. Paul Starbuck—" he sneered as he said Paul's full name "—found that the wall on this end of the house, between the inner and outer layers of brick, contains a very narrow, very steep stairway. An unpleasant place, but useful."

Susannah's eyes widened and her eyebrows went up.

"The top of those stairs is behind that small door in the wainscot. They go down behind the basement wall, where they connect with a tunnel, Susannah. A very solidly built tunnel that goes from the main house to the root cellar beneath the kitchen dependency, where one may enter or exit by moving the shelving along one wall. When I first found this secret passage I never puzzled over its origins, or what it might have been used for. Later, when I returned to Kinloch and found that it was still there and still in excellent condition, I did think about those things. I even did a bit of research. Oh, and by the way, speaking of research—a bit of digression here—I do have your mother's research papers. I took them right from under your father's nose, like stealing candy from a baby. I knew, of course, that he couldn't see well enough to identify me."

Susannah swallowed a gasp.

"And now to resume my story." Marvin leaned forward, enjoying himself as raconteur. "The concealed stairway obviously was included when the house was built. The builder of Laird's Mount took his pattern from great houses he had seen in England or Scotland, and such houses often had a hidden passageway, useful in case the household had to flee some terror in a hurry. Perhaps the tunnel was constructed then, as well. It is equally possible that the stair merely exited into the basement, and that during the time of the Civil War the tunnel was constructed as a means to help runaway slaves escape."

"Fascinating!" said Susannah, for a moment forgetting how dire her situation was.

"Yes, isn't it? Now, as to your unusual ability to draw a picture of me as a boy... I did live in this house. I had a very unhappy youth, Susannah. You would surely pity me if you knew the whole of it." He pouted. He had regained his color, his pouting lips were as shapely and rosy as a woman's, which turned Susannah's stomach.

He went on. "My father was a gambler and a drunkard, and what's more, he murdered my mother. Strangled her, and I saw him do it. Amazing, how the life can go out of a person so quickly. Well. After that he dragged me around the countryside from one place to another. I was afraid of him, of course. I suppose what saved me was that I knew, even when I was a little fellow, that I was smarter than he was. I always managed to go to school wherever we were, and I took books out of the library, or stole them if I had to—I read all the time. He left me alone a lot, you see. But he always locked me in."

Susannah felt called upon to say something. "How awful."

"Yes, it certainly was. Old Dad was not smart, but he was cunning. He always managed to find us a place to live that was isolated, where people would leave us alone. From the time he killed my mother I never had a single friend. We lived here, in this house—I never knew then that it had a name—for just one summer. He kept me locked in almost all the time, in this very room. There was no school in the summer, you see. I ran out of books, and because I was locked in I couldn't get to the library to get more. I was desperate. I think I may have gone quite out of my mind for a time."

"That's understandable," Susannah said, managing to inject a lot of sympathy in her tone.

"I used to sit in that corner there—" he pointed to the very place where she'd had a brief glimpse of the face "—for hours and hours. Days, perhaps. That was when I made the acquaintance of the ghost. There is a ghost, no matter how much you may want to deny it."

Susannah didn't bother to enlighten him with the information she could have given on that subject. Actually, what Marvin was saying had its own strange fascination.

"It never frightened me, I think because we were alike, that ghost and I. Both trapped in this blasted room. But I didn't stay trapped, oh no. I came out of my lethargy and started cleaning up the place, and that

was when I found the little doors. And not long after
that, I found the secret stair and the tunnel."

A pity, thought Susannah, that Daniel Richardson
had never found them!

"And then I did a very brave, very smart thing. I
waited until one night when I was certain Old Dad was
dead drunk—I'd heard him crashing around and
swearing—and I sneaked out of my locked room by
the secret passage and ran away! Now I wish I'd killed
him first, but I was rather puny, not very strong. I
suppose it's just as well I didn't try. I was a very, very
good boy after running away. And lucky, oh yes, I've
always been lucky. I went north, I chose some dinky
little town and got a job sweeping out a store, and another and another, and I went to school, and when I
was sixteen a nice old lady adopted me. She died, with
a little help from me…but you don't need to know all
that. I've told you enough, I think."

Susannah tensed. "Please go on. You've had a very
interesting life, and become so successful!"

"Tsk, tsk. Flattery. You're sounding just like Jane.
But you're not like her at all, are you, Susannah?
However—" he reached in his pocket and took out
two syringes, which he lined up neatly on the table
"—you will die in exactly the same way she did.
Quick, almost painless. No mess."

There was a disturbance downstairs, but Susannah
hardly heard it. The spot behind her right ear stung,
it burned fiercely, and suddenly she saw her mother's
face hanging in the air right in front of her, and in an
instant memories flooded in and came together and it
all made sense. That day in Cambridge, when she'd

thought a spider had bitten her behind the ear, but there was no spider. And she'd gone for a run and come back and found out that her mother was dead...

"What's in the syringes, Marvin? I know you injected my mother in the neck, behind the ear. You *are* smart, that was clever, but then you're a doctor. What do you use?"

"Potassium chloride. Throws the enzymes out of balance, causes the heart to beat erratically, go into spasm, and stop. Injected in exactly the proper place, as you said, behind the ear—how did you know that?" For just a moment his eyes narrowed and he looked disturbed rather than pleased with himself. But his momentum carried him—he was not to be distracted at this point. "A very fine needle, such a tiny prick, leaves almost no mark at all. A pathologist would have to be very suspicious and look very hard to find it. Nobody looked. Not at Jane, and not at Tom Parrish. He was a nasty surprise, Susannah. Not nice of you to have him prowling around. He almost caught me, on the very night I'd come for you! So did that vicious animal of Starbuck's. If I hadn't gone right down in the root cellar and hid in the tunnel until you took the animal away... But never mind."

"*You* killed Tom?" Susannah got her feet under her, bad ankle and all. There had to be some way out of this, there had to be! "And you were the reason Wolf howled that night?"

"Yes," said Marvin succinctly. He picked up one of the syringes and tested it, ejecting a tiny spurt of liquid.

"Wait a minute." Susannah was sure she heard something downstairs. She remembered she'd left one of the back doors open, just the screen closed—but the latch was on the screen. Whatever she'd heard, Marvin didn't hear it. His hands were steady as rock, the expression on his face enrapt as he admired his chosen instrument of death.

Susannah stalled for time. "You can't kill me the way you did Jane and Tom. I'm young, I'm healthy. They'll be suspicious. Paul will find my body, and he'll be sure to call the police. You'll be in trouble, Marvin. You won't get away with it this time!"

"Oh, yes I will," said Marvin, standing up, syringe in hand. "Because no one will find your body. You're going in the tunnel, my dear, and I, under cover of night, will seal up both ends."

"You still won't get Laird's Mount," said Susannah, on her feet now and limping backward, away from him, "because I made a will." She hadn't, she was lying, but she was desperate now. "I left this house to Paul. He put so much time into it, it's as much his as mine."

"I'll have it, it *will* be mine," said Marvin advancing toward her, "because I made a vow the night I ran away from here, that some day I would own this house, this house that saved me from a horrible life! This is *my* house, *mine!*"

From downstairs there was a ripping, tearing sound too loud to ignore, and then a noise like rushing wind. Susannah's head turned, and Marvin froze with his arm and hand holding the syringe in midair. On came the rushing wind and into the room hurdled a black-and-silver bullet of enormous size and strength.

*Wolf!* Susannah thought, collapsing back against the wall.

The dog hit Marvin Bradley square in the chest with such force that she knocked him back three feet, against the wall between the two windows. Susannah heard the expulsion of air forced from Marvin's lungs. He went down, and Wolf was on top of him, growling like a beast from hell, her teeth at his throat. He'd dropped the syringe. Susannah scrambled over and picked it up, and retrieved the other one from the table, too.

Marvin's legs and arms scrabbled. He got enough air back to bleat, "Get it off me, get it off me!"

"If you don't be still and quiet she'll kill you," said Susannah, adding with deadly scorn, "you murderer!"

Just as she began to wonder how long Wolf could hold her prey, and if she herself dared leave the man and the dog to get to a telephone, Susannah heard the sound of tires on gravel. Her heart leapt. She knew Paul had come. Now everything would be all right. Everything.

## *Epilogue*

Marvin Bradley was in jail, the publicity and the scandal had died down, people were wondering what Kinloch was going to do without a doctor, and Paul and Susannah were having one of their arguments.

"If we can have one kind of partnership, I don't see why we can't have another," Paul insisted.

"It's not the same," said Susannah, just as insistent. "It's not the same at all."

"Well, of course it isn't. My kind's more fun."

"For you, maybe."

He trapped her in his arms. "For both of us. Wolf, too. She loves you almost as much as I do."

Susannah let him kiss her, then she kissed him back. "Mmm. Paul Starbuck and his magical, wonderful Wolf. I owe my life to you two."

"Don't talk about that," Paul said, crushing her to his chest. "I can't stand to think about it."

"Wolf came, and so did you."

"Without her, I might have been too late."

"No, you wouldn't." Susannah raised her face in a way that she'd learned would invite Paul to kiss her again, and he did. "You knew that I was in danger. It's mysterious and wonderful and I don't understand it. Somehow you knew, and you came!"

"I knew because I love you, and I want you to marry me. Wolf wants you to marry me. Come on, Susannah, say yes."

She moved back, taking Paul's hands and teasing him. "We will be partners. You already agreed. Hathaway and Starbuck, Restorations."

"Starbuck and Starbuck," said Paul stubbornly, but he was smiling. His eyes were full of love. "And someday it will be Starbuck and Starbuck *and* Starbuck."

Susannah put her hands over her ears. "I can't stand it!"

"And Starbuck. To the nth degree. Lots and lots of little Starbucks growing to be big Starbucks, all restoring things."

"I swear, I just can't stand it!"

"All you have to do to get me to stop is say yes."

Susannah removed her hands from her ears and planted them on her hips. She tossed her head, gray eyes shining. There was a mischievious note in her voice. "I won't be a victim of blackmail, Paul."

He looked crushed.

Then she smiled. "Well, actuallly I would. And I will. Yes, yes, YES!"

**Relive the romance...
Harlequin and Silhouette
are proud to present**

*by Request*

A program of collections of three complete novels by the most requested authors with the most requested themes. Be sure to look for one volume each month with three complete novels by top name authors.

In June: **NINE MONTHS** Penny Jordan
Stella Cameron
Janice Kaiser

**Three women pregnant and alone. But a lot can happen in nine months!**

In July: **DADDY'S HOME** Kristin James
Naomi Horton
Mary Lynn Baxter

**Daddy's Home... and his presence is long overdue!**

In August: **FORGOTTEN PAST** Barbara Kaye
Pamela Browning
Nancy Martin

**Do you dare to create a future if you've forgotten the past?**

Available at your favorite retail outlet.

HARLEQUIN    Silhouette

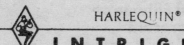

## HARLEQUIN®

# I N T R I G U E®

Hop into a pink Cadillac with the King of Rock 'n' Roll for the hottest—most mysterious—August of 1993 ever!

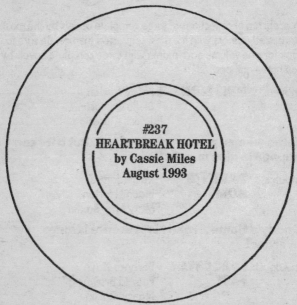

#237
HEARTBREAK HOTEL
by Cassie Miles
August 1993

All Susan Quentin wanted was a quiet birthday, but she got lots more: sexy greetings over the radio, deejay Johnny Swift himself—and a dead Elvis impersonator outside her door. Armed with only sunglasses and a pink Cadillac, could they find the disguised "King" killer amid a convention of impersonators at the Heartbreak Hotel?

Don't be cruel! Come along for the ride of your life when Johnny tries to convince Susan to love him tender!

ELVIS

# HARLEQUIN®

# INTRIGUE®

## "I AM BETRAYED"

In the still of the night, those were the words spoken to
Emma Devlin by her husband, Frank . . . from beyond the
grave. She'd given him no cause to doubt her devotion, yet he
haunted her waking hours and disturbed her dreams.

Next month, Harlequin Intrigue brings you a chilling tale of
love and disloyalty . . .

### #241 FLESH AND BLOOD
### by Caroline Burnes
### September 1993

In an antebellum mansion, Emma finds help from the oddest of
sources: in the aura of a benevolent ghost—and in the arms of
a gallant Confederate colonel.

For a spine-tingling story about a love that transcends time,
don't miss Harlequin Intrigue #241 FLESH AND BLOOD,
coming to you in September.